W9-ADK-005

JO SILVER

BOOKS BY ROBERT NEWTON PECK

A Day No Pigs Would Die

Path of Hunters

Millie's Boy

Soup

Fawn

Wild Cat

Bee Tree (poems)

Soup and Me

Hamilton

Hang for Treason

Rabbits and Redcoats

King of Kazoo (a musical)

Trig

Last Sunday

The King's Iron

Patooie

Soup for President

Eagle Fur

Trig Sees Red

Basket Case

Hub

Mr. Little

Clunie

Soup's Drum

Secrets of Successful Fiction

Trig Goes Ape

Soup on Wheels

Justice Lion

Kirk's Law

Trig or Treat

Banjo

Soup in the Saddle

Fiction is Folks

The Seminole Seed

Soup's Goat

Dukes

Spanish Hoof

Jo Silver

Soup on Ice

JO SILVER

by
Robert Newton Peck

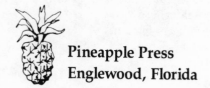

Pineapple Press
Englewood, Florida

CURR
PZ
7
P339
.Jo
1985

Library of Congress Cataloging in Publication Data

Peck, Robert Newton.
    Jo Silver.

    Summary: Sixteen-year-old Kenny's hike through the Adirondacks in
search of a writer at Lost Pond becomes a fight for survival as he realizes
he is not alone in the hostile wilderness.
    [1. Hiking—Fiction.   2. Survival—Fiction.
3. Adirondack Mountains (N.Y.)—Fiction]   I. Title.
PZ7.P339Jo   1985   [Fic]   85-3720
ISBN 0-910923-20-5

Composition by Miller Typography, Jacksonville, Florida
Printing by Fairfield Graphics, Fairfield, Pennsylvania

ACKNOWLEDGMENT

Please allow me here to salute two new friends of mine, Phyles and Philip Crosby of Philip Crosby Associates. They are furthering quality of American life far more than I ever could.

1

The bus stopped.

As its brakes hissed, the husky driver turned on the foam pad upon which he sat to look at me. I was the only Adirondack Trailways passenger.

"This is it, sonny. Pine Corners. End of the line, and if you ask me, the end of the world." He halfway smiled.

My legs felt stiff, and my left foot tingled with sleep as I spun up and out of my seat. Hauling my large orange backpack down from the overhead rack, I saddled myself into it. The pack weighed about sixty pounds. Almost half my own skinny weight of one hundred and thirty.

Cap off, the driver squinted at me. "Boy," he said, "you're not one of them runaways, are ya?"

I shot him a friendly grin for his concern. "Not me. I like my folks. My name's Kenny Matson, and I'm from Stamford, Connecticut." As I shuffled forward to wait at the door of the bus, I sensed he wasn't going to crack it open without one or two more questions. His ruddy face was rounder than a pizza, and curious.

1

"You're kind of a long way from home, ain't cha? It's October," he told me. "And it's also a Wednesday. If you ain't running away, how come you ain't in school?"

In a way, I was tempted to tell the bus driver about the crackling debate I'd had, just last evening, with both of my parents. A telephone call. Mom was on the kitchen phone while Dad chimed in from the red telephone in the den. We all jabbered like fury and nobody listened to anybody. It was sort of fun; because in the end, I won.

"I'm in prep school," I told the bus driver, "where I got on the bus, in Lake Placid. I go to North Academy. But I'm taking a few days off."

"How come? To coondog after some *girl*?"

His question made me almost flinch. "Well," I said, "to *find somebody*." I shifted my weight onto the needles of my awakening toes. "You can report me to the state troopers if it will ease your conscience. I don't mind."

His chubby body sighed inside the gray uniform. "Kids," he said. "They never like it where they are. Hobos."

I wasn't in the mood for a lecture on the shortcomings of today's youth. So I said, "Please open the door. I'm in kind of a hurry."

"Okay." His hand rested on the door release. "You sure ya know where you're headed? The Adirondacks is a big hunk of real estate. Especially up here."

The door folded open, squeaking, parting its black rubbery lips. But as I stepped off, I twisted around. "Thanks."

"For what? You paid for your ticket."

"If it'll ease your worrying, I'm hiking up to a place called Lost Pond. Dad and I go hunting a lot, so I'm not scared of the wilderness."

The driver consulted his wristwatch. "I gotta git rolling. When I'm late for supper, the wife rents out my room." He chuckled. "Be careful up in all them mountains. Take caution."

I smiled at him. "I promise to. So long."

"So long, kid, and good hunting. I hope ya locate the person you're searching for."

I was itching to ask him if he'd ever heard of Jo Silver. But then the doors slammed and the big diesel belched a cloud of black exhaust. The yellow and red Trailways bus turned around and went wheezing away as though it couldn't wait to leave town.

I looked around.

Pine Corners wasn't much of a village. Nearly deserted. Yet I'd visited dozens like it in northern Vermont and also here in upstate New York. Pine Corners seemed to be mostly one main street, a few stores. One of the signs said Clepp's Hardware.

This store was my starting place. Because back at school, Dr. Gray, who was my favorite teacher, somehow knew of Mr. Clepp, and had begged me to check in with him upon my arrival at Pine Corners.

Entering the store, I heard a tiny bell announce my presence as I carefully closed the door. I looked around. Buffalo plaid woolens in checkerboard red and green hung on racks. There were rows of shotguns and rifles, plus a well-stocked ammunition case beside the camping equipment. From behind a far counter, a lean and almost bald proprietor studied me over his halfmoon glasses. His face was square and his body angular, as if he had stepped into life from a needlepoint sampler.

"Are you Mr. Clepp?"

"Yup. At least I was this morning," he said through his nose. "Can I help ya?"

I nodded. "I'm wondering, sir, if you'd be so kind as

3

to advise me on the best route to Lost Pond."

Mr. Clepp's eyes narrowed. "You just took yourself off'n the noon bus." The man was no fool.

"That's right."

"You ain't got no vehicle."

"No. I'm hiking."

Before saying more, Mr. Clepp dusted off his brown wooden counter with a dirty rag. Then he gave a tug to one of the black arm garters which pinched the upper sleeves of his pale work shirt. Perhaps his shirt had once been blue, many washings ago.

"Nothin' much up there, boy."

I didn't argue. "On my map," I said, "it appears to be about ten miles west of Pine Corners. Is that correct?"

"Ten miles? Well, maybe so and maybe no. There ain't a road."

"Well, as you said, I don't have a vehicle. So I don't suppose I'll be needing a road of any kind."

Mr. Clepp snorted. "I lived here all my life. Sixty years. And there's plenty of fellas, growed-up ones, that've looked for Lost Pond and never found it."

I smiled. "Maybe that's how it earned the name."

"S'pose so."

"I still want to go. I have to."

"How come?"

"I'm searching for something." I was careful not to say *someone*. "That's all."

"You from down country?"

My pack wasn't light. And I didn't feel in the mood to share my secret with Mr. Clepp. Perhaps, I was thinking, it had been a mistake to tell the bus driver, even though he'd seemed to be a friendly cuss.

"As I see it, sir," I said, trying to sound polite as well as patient, "it's not where I'm from that matters. It's where I'm going."

4

"Lost Pond, eh?"

"Yup," I said, holding back a laugh.

With a shrug, Mr. Clepp pointed a lean finger. "For starters, I'd follow the road outa town that passes by a long row of popple trees and then the Methodist Church. Ya can't miss it."

I felt confused. "I didn't think there was a road. You said..."

"Ain't. The road quits in maybe half a mile, right after you go by Bessie Quill's place. Beyond that, you're on you own."

I grinned. "I don't know Miss Quill."

Mr. Clepp grunted. "Too bad. Most men do."

I laughed, even though Mr. Clepp resisted, his Yankee face remaining immune from even his own humor.

"When the road stops, what do I do then?"

"There's a trail. It don't go nowhere. But it's a free country, so I s'pose you can follow it a spell, if you're a mind to."

"And it goes to Lost Pond?"

Mr. Clepp wiped his bifocals on the front of his shirt. "Some claim it should. Others claim no. Suit yourself."

"Thanks a lot, Mr. Clepp."

"Don't mention it. And don't expect to git too far before sundown. It's already noon. Dark comes sudden up yonder. It'll be steep. Uphill most of the way, they tell me. Maybe you'd best wiser wait until morning and cut yourself a fresh start."

"Okay," I said, though I wasn't planning to wait. "Is there a supermarket in Pine Corners?"

"Nope. Used to be, years back. But when the sawmill shut down for keepers, it went too. There's a grocer across the street. You can tell Libby I sentcha."

"Libby?" I started to leave.

Mr. Clepp hooked on his glasses. "Oh, she owns it.

5

Libby Potter. Ya can't miss her. She's about the size of a barn and smells worse."

I laughed again.

"By the way, you got a compass? One might fetch handy once ya trudge yourself up into the nowheres."

I didn't have one and I told him so. Reaching under his counter, he brought out a compass and blew off its dust.

"Here's one. Only a dollar and two bits."

I examined the bargain compass, watching the quivering needle seesaw on its pivot. Then I fished out the money and paid him his price, hearing the grateful jangle of his gold-colored cash register after he had punched down the keys.

He eyed my pack. "You got some burden to tote uphill. Looks bigger'n you be. How old are ya?"

"I'm sixteen."

"Well, if ya hanker to meet up with seventeen, I wouldn't stray up in the yonder too long. Or too far. And by the way, boy, they say there's lode in those mountains."

"Lode?"

Mr. Clepp nodded. "Iron ore. Enough to spin a compass crazier than cheap whiskey. Can't tell north from your hind end. Got a knife?"

I had one. It was my hunting knife attached, in a leather sheath, to my belt. I showed it to him. As he looked at it, he nudged the cash drawer back into the register, using his stomach.

"Good. Notch a tree or two on your way west. Hear? Thataway, at least you'll know where ya been, once you decide ya don't know where ya are."

"Good advice. I'll take it."

"What if she rains?"

"I have a slicker. Plus a nylon slipover for my sleeping

bag. I'll be dryer than toast."

Grunting his disbelief, Mr. Clepp ambled around from the counter to walk me as far as his jingling door. "Well," he said, "ya got more spunk than brains. I'll say that much for ya."

"Thanks. I'll be okay. Unless I stop in to tarry a few pleasant moments with Miss Quill."

He clapped me on the shoulder. "Whoa yourself in here on the way back so I'll know ya made it. Hear?"

"I will."

"*If* you make it."

2

Mr. Clepp had been correct.

Across the street from his hardware establishment, Libby Potter almost filled her tiny grocery. Perhaps the apron she wore had once been white; but now it was little more than an overall brown smudge, a color which matched her dress, her complexion, and the entire climate of her store. Even the air smelled brown.

Sizing me up as a stranger, her weasel eyes followed my every move as I selected a loaf of bread, a small cooked ham, a sack of white beans, a tiny jar of instant coffee, plus several yellow apples.

She watched me ruin the bread, or so she must have thought, as I compressed it like an accordian, to stuff into my backpack.

"You nuts?" she asked me.

I nodded. Then I added three Milky Ways, a Baby Ruth and a Snicker. If you're still a kid, I was thinking, adults usually presume that you don't know what you're doing, and you won't survive even one more second without their advice or their prying. From the looks of

8

Libby Potter, I'd guess she couldn't have interrogated a roach. Yet it didn't hold her back.

"You one of them environment loonies?"

"That's me." I broke out into a chuckle. "Wherever I go, there's always lots of environment."

Libby nodded. "Figured as much. Hey, ya better not salt all them purchases away until I total up whatcha owe me."

I smiled. "Okay. What's the damage?"

Without a formal reply, Libby Potter's pencil stub started a crude column of numbers on a folded brown bag. I could see that mathematics, even in the simplest form, had not been her best subbject. Her calculation was far from speedy.

Finally she surrendered a sigh. "Ten bucks even."

"Fair enough."

Even though I presumed it was no better than an estimate, in her favor, I yanked a ten from my wallet. As I did so, I watched her eyes checking to see how much money I had left. Her face seemed to betray her regret in not saying eleven. Pine Corners, from what little I had seen of it, appeared to be untouched by prosperity. In both the hardware store and her grocery, I observed, I'd been the lone customer.

"Maybe," she said, fingering my ten-dollar bill, "I made a mistake."

I moved quickly. "Possibly. Here, let me total it up for you. If it'll add up to less than ten, I'll get change coming."

Her nostrils flared. Caught with her greed showing, Libby retreated, forced a half smile and shrugged her monstrous shoulders. She even faked a sullen glance down to her figures on the bag.

"Nope," she said, "I got it right. Ten even."

I didn't smile. The Libby Potters of the world stayed

on their own turf, sometimes having troublesome relatives who owned guns, I was thinking. She'd already taken me for a buck or two, so I wasn't about to wipe the smirk of a petty victory from her puffy face.

"You win," I said for insurance.

Losers, I had earlier decided, like to be told that they're winners. It was plain to behold that old Libby hadn't *won* much during her shabby life in Pine Corners. So today I'd let her wear the gold.

She tossed the bill into a cigar box.

"New to town, are ya?"

"Just passing through."

"Where to?"

Watching me pack my food, Libby was suddenly acting too friendly, too interested; not in me or my purpose, yet perhaps in my wallet. It was time to lie a defense.

"I'm meeting friends of my dad, all hunters, sometime later today. I'm from Lake Placid. But we come up here hunting a lot. You have real nice people in this town, like Mr. Clepp, across the street."

Libby Potter rested big hands on bigger hips. "I seen you alight off'n the noon bus. You was all by your lonesome."

I nodded. Yet I didn't change my story. Quickly I added, "You haven't seen a big Buick wagon with a gunrack pull into town yet, have you?"

She shook her head, perhaps suspecting there would be no Buick and no friends. I continued to stuff my overpriced chow under the top flap of my pack, as the portly groceress of Pine Corners studied me. "On a vacation, are ya?"

"Sort of. My father's friend is a rifle expert. High-powered stuff. He's going to show me how to shoot a moose gun tomorrow. I can't wait." All of this was bold-faced fiction.

"Where ya stayin' in town?"

"We're not. As I said, we're just passing through. To enjoy your beautiful October."

As Libby sat on her counter, the wood groaned. "It's too early for deer season. That don't come until late November. As for moose, nobody's sighted none in *my* lifetime. Up in Canada, yeah. Not around these here parts."

All I wanted to do was to strap down my pack, load up, and get away from Libby Potter's persistent questioning. I regretted my error in mentioning Lost Pond to Mr. Clepp, even though he and Libby seemed, to me, to be opposites in nature. One thing certain, I wasn't going to mention the name Jo Silver. Not to anyone. Nor was I about to inquire where Jo Silver Fox was hiding out. Besides, a lot of this trip was too personal to share. My parents and Dr. Gray knew. That's enough. I'd leaked far too much already.

Hoisting my load to my back, I struggled to poke my arm through the second strap. Libby Potter made no move to help.

"You won't be hikin' too distant saddled under all that gear," she told me. "No skinny link like you."

"I suppose not."

"Not far and not fast."

I took it all with a mental shrug. People like Libby Potter who never exercised much, didn't jog, never played tennis, had little conception of my stamina. No idea of how long I could drive my one hundred and thirty puny pounds. For her, a waddle from one wall of her dreary grocery to the other would be an expedition. Most of her world, I concluded, was this one dismal room.

Had she ever been, I wondered, anywhere other than

Pine Corners? No car would easily hold her. It would have to be at least a pickup truck. Obviously, she was in love with her fork. Yet inside, I couldn't point a cruel finger and laugh at her. I felt sincerely sorry for Libby and the limited life she led.

"You're right," I told her. "I'll be very grateful to see my friends pull into town in that big Buick."

"I bet. How come ya ain't with em?"

Libby was brighter than she looked. She almost *had* to be. I was beginning to learn an important lesson; that being, people who appear to be stupid not always are. She sensed something was up.

"We just decided to meet here. That's all." I hoped it would be enough to satisfy Libby as I finally got my backpack on.

As I turned to leave, my brain was firing off a dozen questions. I doubted that someone as uneducated as Libby Potter had ever heard of Jo Silver. But had Jo Silver Fox ever ventured down from Lost Pond to Pine Corners? Perhaps the large lady in a dirty apron knew the way to Lost Pond. Would I be a fool to ask her?

"Hey!"

Hearing her voice almost bark, I turned, to see her pointing a fat finger at me.

"You city people think we're all dumber than monkeys up here. Well, we ain't. Don't figure that you're the first bigshot downroader that's ever hit town. Not by a bug's measure."

Looking at her, I understood. She had asked me questions and I had answered them all in an evasive way. Worse yet, I'd shamefully lied. Maybe, I thought, I was just a lousy liar. Out of practice; because, prior to this adventurous mission, I'd never really had much cause to lie.

"Humpf," she snorted. "You greenhorns is all alike."

"If I offended you, in any way, I apologize. I'm not a bigshot. I came in here to be a cash customer. That's all. I didn't come into your store to be mean or to be rude."

"What's your name, sonny."

"John Smith," I blurted out.

As I did so, my guts winced at my obvious simplicity. Looking at the counter, I saw a Milky Way that I had somehow overlooked. But as I went to retrieve it, Libby Potter shot out her hand, snatched it, ripped off its dusty paper, and then bit away a good half.

I felt sweaty. And angry.

Twisting my head, I saw the half-filled box of Milky Ways on one of her shelves. Would I do it? Did I have the courage to stroll over, take one, and then casually leave? I wanted to. Sanity prevented. Let her win a round, I decided, and enjoy a candy bar that I had purchased.

"You win," I said to her again.

Turning, I opened the door and was halfway through it when I heard Libby Potter say a few more words. She didn't yell. Instead, her voice was steady, almost as though she really was a momentary victor. Yet her farewell growl nearly froze my heart.

"*You* won't find no pond."

3

Steady, I warned myself.

Leaving the grocery store, I was careful to turn right, not left. Then, ducking up an alley, I doubled back, passing behind some shabby buildings and a few houses, until I was finally headed west.

I passed the Methodist Church.

"Why the charade?" I asked myself aloud. No wonder some of the guys at school considered me a nerd. I was acting like one, I told myself. You're not fooling anyone. Wrong! I was probably fooling dumb old Kenny Matson into believing that Libby Potter didn't know where I was going. How, I asked myself, had she found out?

The telephone!

I remembered having taken two or three minutes, just looking around, as I had crossed the street from the hardware store to the grocery. Mr. Clepp had telephoned her, no doubt. I'd spotted a phone on her counter. Not having spied a telephone in Clepp's Hardware surely didn't mean he didn't have one.

"You're a prize oaf, Matson," I said, feeling as if I

was now being observed by every eye in town.

The reputed half a mile from the Pine Corners First Methodist Church all the way to the residence of the well-known Miss Bessie Quill, seemed to be closer to a mile. A country mile, mostly uphill. I noticed the faded red door on her house and smiled.

Should I go up and knock?

"Howdo, Miss Quill," I imagined myself to say. "You may have heard about me from some of your in-town associates. I'm John Smith, the famous lover of Lake Placid."

"Why of course," she'd say. "There's not a lady, young *or* old, in Pine Corners who hasn't heard of you, Mr. Smith. Why, I declare, you could be my favorite John."

I eked out a weak giggle. Matson, I was thinking as I hiked by the red-door residence with a Q on its mailbox, at least you haven't lost your levity.

Back at school, that's what Dr. Gray always said in Biology. "We'd all go nuts if we don't crack a smile." He was a great old gent, Dr. Abraham Gray. The guys all called him Honest Abe because he'd excuse almost any variety of horseplay or deviltry, except *cheating* on a quiz. Or peeking.

I looked ahead.

Mr. Clepp, he of hardware fame, had certainly told me the truth. The road stopped. The dirt road and all its pebbles merely melted into a stand of rusted autumn weeds. And to a path. To be more accurate, two paths, as though originally cut by wagon wheels.

Looking back as I walked, I saw the housetops of Pine Corners sink into the flaming October foliage of the Adirondacks and disappear.

"Here I go," I said, recalling a hunk of advice that Dr. Gray had given us one time in class. "Never," he'd said, "allow formal education to stunt your growth."

Pity, I thought, that I hadn't stopped at Miss Bessie Quill's modest little establishment of horizontal refreshment. If she'd answered the door, I'd probably have turned tail and split. Never had I seen a hooker, up close. They were no doubt like the rest of us. I was certain they didn't look like Martians.

"No, no, Miss Quill," I said aloud in my lowest baritone, "I'm not really John Smith, the world-famous lover. In fact, I am Kenneth Matson from North Academy, and I've only kissed one girl in my entire sixteen years. Her name's Amy."

Why, I wondered, do I talk to myself whenever I'm feeling a bit nervous? Libby Potter was right. I'm nuts. Maybe I should have explained to dear old Libby that baking corporations, who bake bread, also package in a lot more air than wheat flour. So, a hiker who's packing his own grub squeezes out all the air to take up less space. It all tastes the same.

I hiked by an enormous weeping willow tree, a russet fountain, cascading some secret sorrow like the head of a heartbroken giant. Vines covered the roadside bushes, their yellowing October leaves still thicker than roof shingles. Beyond the row of bushes lay an open field, where a pair of gray squirrels were dragging an unharvested ear of corn through the stubble. A dead tree on my right supported a woodpecker who was busily tapping, telegraphing his warning message to the insects.

Several crows, I counted seven, argued on the roof of a deserted barn, a black minstrel show, perhaps discussing some local scandal in their small community. Near the barn stood an old gray horse who looked as though he'd outlived his trot.

Ahead, the wagon road seemed to be still winding northwest. I checked my new compass as well as the sun which was frying my left shoulder. Lode? It was iron ore, Mr. Clepp said. As for right now, my compass seemed to be on target and properly functioning.

I'd sort of liked Mr. Clepp. Maybe, old as he was, he'd someday marry Libby Potter. Then they could combine their inventory. Ha! All under one roof to cut expenses. Knowing the lady grocer as I did, and her elastic standards of commercial integrity, they could call their new place of business The Clepp Joint.

I hadn't noticed where I was walking. Ahead, the two-rut wagon road had strangely diminished into a single upward path, too narrow for a wagon. And much too rocky. Big granite tumors of rough gray sprouted up from brown quilts of pine needles, more still than a flock of sleeping ewes.

Goldenrod seemed to be growing almost everywhere, their brassy-fingered hands all stretching upward like a classroom of elementary scholars, all of whom were eager to answer a teacher's question. Along with the goldenrod grew milkweed, now brown, standing as a sorority of flossy-headed hags with hairy heads of unruly white floss. I could see the dark dots of escaping seeds.

My compass read due west.

I wanted to sneak another look at my map, but it was folded, deep inside my backpack. No need, actually. All I had to do was keep walking to the west. Dad said that trails always lead to somewhere. Often as not, he'd added, to water of some variety...a creek or a pond. Eventually, an ocean. But that was true only for hiking downhill. My path was *up*.

I grinned.

My mind was picturing the scene at home, last evening, right after their two overheated telephones had returned to their cradles. I bet both Mom and Dad chattered a purple streak. Yet they knew it was time for me to atttempt one important mission in my life, that being, to find Jo Silver Fox. I'd often threatened to do it. What had held me back was that I didn't quite know how. Or where to look.

Now I knew. Because of the book.

As my back was cramping, I yanked off my big orange load to take a one-minute breather. No more. My instinct could warn me when sixty seconds had wasted. I sat on a rock, remembering last year and the book I'd found. It had been resting, among others, in a large box, upstairs in the North Academy Library. These semi-destroyed books were destined to be thrown out. Yet there it was.

My Sky, by John S. Fay.

Some careless reader had torn off its hard outer cover, in front. Only its guts remained. So I started reading page one, more out of pity than interest. I just felt sorry to see a book so ravaged and so naked. Even though I'm a hungry reader, I had never heard of its author, Mr. John S. Fay. But it really grabbed me, right away.

I stole the book.

Stuffing it up under my NORTH sweatshirt, I sneaked out of the library. That night, I had stayed up until way after two o'clock, reading it. Before I had read halfway through the book, I knew one thing for certain. I'd have bet my life on it.

John S. Fay was *not* its author.

On top of that, I was guessing who *had* written *My Sky*. It had been written by a writer and a scholar with whose works I was more than familiar, thanks to the original urging of Dr. Gray. So, going back to the library, I fingered through the card catalog, looking for other titles by John S. Fay. I found not a one. Only *My Sky*.

Then I was sure.

My Sky had been written by Jo Silver Fox. Same initials: J.S.F. The wording, phrases, style...all Jo Silver's.

No one else's. Most of all, it was the book's *philosophy* that convinced me. It was a lofty and birdlike freedom which humans, animals, and plants were given by God.

The mystery was haunting me. Why had Jo Silver Fox written *My Sky* under a fake name? Digging a bit deeper, I had then discovered that there was no such person as John S. Fay. No author data in *Contemporary Writers*. Yet there were scraps of information about Jo Silver Fox. Not at all complete. But what was strange about the data on Jo Silver was this. All of it was old. At least twenty or thirty years.

Nothing current.

About a week after I had ripped off the book, *My Sky*, I picked it up again, in my room at North Academy. In the very back of the old book was a library envelope, glued to a back page. Inside, a tiny newspaper clipping had been wedged; it was yellow and dry with age, and I had to unfold it carefully. It was about the nearby town of Pine Corners. And it mentioned the name of somebody I now had to find.

Jo Silver Fox, the writer of the article suspected, now lived as a recluse, near a place called Lost Pond.

4

I half-peeled a Milky Way.

Shouldering my heavy orange pack, I legged it uphill along the winding path, munching my energy and inhaling balsam and cedar.

The day was becoming partly cloudy and overcast. Looking upward through a gap in the green pines, I saw a crow circling, penciling his black circles on a gray sky. It reminded me of *My Sky*, the book in my backpack. For a moment, I wanted to be a crow, tasting the October wind, able to look downward on a vividly painted Adirondack mountain autumn.

"You're lucky," I told the crow.

Finishing the last of my candy bar, I tossed its brown wrapper to the pine needles at my feet. But then I stopped. Bending, I picked it up, stuffing the crumpled wrapper into a pocket of my parka. It wasn't just the trivial sin of littering that plagued me. More than that, it was the face of the Pine Corners groceress, Libby Potter. So, I had decided, there was no reason to leave a trail marker. Just in case she had a few scruffy pals who, by now, were aware of my carrying a gifted wallet.

"Don't panic," I told myself. However, regarding the candy wrapper, it made little sense to court trouble. Pine Corners probably was a town of good people. But surely not all of them were above temptation and an easy score. It was a gun town. Just as Mr. Clepp's establishment was a gun store, one of lethal hardware.

My path stopped.

Suddenly I was aware that I'd been walking through the trees, following nothing. No trail. As had the gravel road near Miss Bessie Quill's, the path had quietly quit. I fished out my compass. Well, I thought upon reading it, I'm still facing west. And going uphill. Mr. Clepp had warned that I would be hiking *up* all the way. That I had expected.

How far had I come, I wondered. My guess was about four to five miles. Yet possibly less. Looking up, I saw the crow no longer. As a crow flies, I thought, ten miles to Lost Pond.

My map I had practically memorized.

Pulling out my hunting knife, I notched a spruce. Maybe it was a hemlock. I wasn't too certain nor did I honestly give a hoot. At least, I was thinking, a freshly cut patch on a tree trunk wouldn't be as obvious as a Milky Way wrapper which lay on a trail bed.

Unshouldering my pack, I rested, eating an apple. This, I promised, would be my final splurge as a late lunch. No snacks. No pigging out at a McDonald's on burgers, shakes, or fries. Not up here. My grub poke, as Dad often called it, would have to linger and last.

Last year, I had started to collect maps of Adirondack counties, but noticed no Pine Corners on any of them. Finally I found the town on a newer map; yet, among the cluster of small bodies of water, there was no Lost

Pond. Until, using a magnifying glass which I borrowed from our North Academy librarian, I finally spotted a tiny irregular circle, within which had been printed the initials L.P. The cartographer who had mapped the area, his map proved, had either a degree of honesty or a sense of humor. Because, following the L.P. was a minute question mark.

It was, I was now thinking as I tasted Milky Way in my mouth, the smallest yet largest question mark in my life.

Above my head, I heard a chirping then saw a chickadee perched on a pine branch.

"Howdy," I said. "I'm here because I've been told never to allow formal education to stunt my growth. Which way to Lost Pond?"

He, or she, didn't answer me. The bird must have concluded that my conversation was a bore; it took off, disappearing into the shadows.

The October afternoon was darkening. I expected it. Once the sun crept over these mountains, night would hide me completely. I wondered about whether or not I should later risk a fire to boil my beans. I'd had no lunch. Only a Milky Way and the apple that I was now biting. It was a yellow Delicious. I ate the entire apple, core and all, except for the stem. I spat out a few seeds. At home, or at school, I wouldn't have eaten an apple so frugally. Here, things were different. It mattered to conserve strength, nutrition, and sanity.

It was fear that I dreaded the most.

As I reshouldered my backpack, I wondered just how much bowel I would have when night came. I wasn't lost. Not yet. Finding my way back downhill to Pine Corners would be, I hoped, a leadpipe cinch. At least my legs weren't aching. They felt tough, strong, willing to tackle the Adirondack wilderness. I had bought a pamphlet once. It was called "Why the Wilderness Is Called Adirondack" and written by a man, years ago, named Henry Dornburgh.

I nodded. Perhaps that was the reason I so often thought of these Adirondacks and wilderness as being one and the same. Dad claimed that Ad-iron-dack was a Mohawk name, meaning *Where Iron Is*. It made me wonder if Dad and Mr. Clepp were somehow secretly in cahoots.

I came to a dry creekshed.

No sign of water. Damn it! I had forgotten my canteen. Well, no going back to North Academy now. My father always stated that *something* always is forgotten on every hike. On every hunting or fishing trip. Because, he said, hikers are only human. On the phone, last evening, he'd said, "The three most important rules are these: Know where you're going, where you are, and how to get back."

That little jewel of a comment had prompted Mom to explode. "You actually mean you're telling him he should *go*?"

Then they argued. I listened. All it did was run up their telephone bill, but I thought, at least from my end at Lake Placid, it was a real kicker.

"Sam Matson," my mother had nearly screamed, "I can't *believe* you'd tell your only child to chase up to some lost lake, or whatever it's called, to hunt up some...*hermit*."

"Easy now, Shirl," Dad had said. "He wants to do it. And I say let him. Ken's been in the woods dozens of times. He'll be..."

"Alone?" my mother shrieked.

They were three hundred miles away; so my parents, neither one of them, could actually forbid me to go. Or, to be more accurate, prevent my going. I told them where and I told them why. At home, during my last summer's vacation, I'd bent their ears about Jo Silver Fox and about *My Sky*. So they both knew that my finding the writer whom I worshipped meant a lot to me. Plus the fact that I promised to telephone them by late Sunday evening. If not, Dad had warned, he'd telephone the New York State Police barracks, near Pine Corners.

Creeks always fascinate me. Mainly because at only one viewing spot, a woodsman can see so little of it, merely a brief segment, like an inch that's chopped from the middle of a lengthy snake. You can't see its source or its destiny. My father's advice came to mind. "Kenny, if you're ever lost, or even suspect you are, follow a stream. Even if it's only a trickle, or dead dry. Water always flows to people, as we humans rarely stray too distant from our amphibian spawning. Every manjack of us is three quarters water."

Making sure I walked uphill, I followed the dried-up creek bed for about a quarter of a mile. For good reason. Mountain brooks don't just happen. They come from either a spring or a *pond*. The fern growth told me that it was a spring. So did the shine of wet rocks. Ferns always congregate near springs, like little girls in the green lace of party dresses who somehow cannot dance without wet feet.

I found it.

Kneeling, I took long sips from the wee pocket of water that was, even in October, little warmer than liquid ice. It burned my teeth and throat. Forcing myself, I drank far more than I wanted or needed. Indians, I had heard, would boil roots in their own urine. Well, maybe I wasn't quite ready to try that. Not so soon. Pulling the cooking kit from my pack, I filled the saucepan by spitting mouthfuls of cold water into it. I counted.

It took twenty. Enough, I figured, to boil a few beans for an after-dark supper. Maybe some coffee first.

There I'd be, I thought, huddled in the dark around my own cozy, perhaps risky, campfire.

I smiled. Ken Matson, I told myself, you *do* have a brain. I would merely boil my beans *now*, before dark, when a small fire wouldn't betray my location. Just in case one or two of the Pine Corners townies had notions about the bread in my wallet.

Pack off, I reached into a fallen log for three handfuls of dry tinder. Almost dust, it smelled of cedar. And it would emit little smoke.

I couldn't find my matches.

But then, as my arm sank deep to the bottom of my pack, my fingertip was rewarded. I knew I'd packed them. They had only settled as I had hiked. Dad had told me this happens a lot to a hiker. "It can cause panic," he'd said, "which can be a lone woodsman's worst enemy."

"Dad," I said, "you're an okay guy."

Using only dry twigs, to prevent any telltale smoke, I boiled and ate some of my beans. Only forty, as I estimated the bag to contain perhaps two hundred. Being sensible pleased me; and, inside my belly, I felt a bit like smirking my maturity. I also ate some ham.

Using two slices of mashed bread, I wiped the bean gravy out of the inside of my saucepan. And I cleaned my spoon in the same manner. Then, with my one tiny bar of hotel soap, I scrubbed the utensils clean, rinsing them with one precious spit of spring water, and finally steamed both spoon and pan to sterility over my tiny fire.

"Matson," I said, "you really know what you're doing, even alone." I tried to sound convincing.

It was dusk.

Yet I wasn't afraid. Not even one goose bump. The evening was quiet, as an earlier October frost had, I figured, killed or hibernated most of the bugs which one might hear in summer. This was good. Being a light sleeper, I'd easily be able to hear anything, or anyone, stalking my way.

I unrolled my sleeping bag. Beneath it, I heaped a thick mat of dry pine needles, for comfort's sake. All I had to do, I thought, unzipping the bag, was to constantly recall what Dad and I did in the woods. And play it all like a really cool dude. Carefully I unlaced my boots, so as not to knot a lace in the dark. I would sleep in my socks and clothes.

As soon as I had scattered the embers of the tiny cooking fire, I crept into my bag, beneath its nylon rain sheet, in case. Lying on my side, I watched a dozen red eyes, tiny fire coals, softly fade to red-gray, then sleep in their warm bed.

"There's nothing to fear," I whispered.

5

I couldn't sleep.

Perhaps, I thought as I stared into the quiet darkness, the bones were too tired and the brain too excited.

It was easy to imagine that Mom was awake, three hundred or more miles away, in Stamford. I pictured her lying there, tossing, punching her pillow, and possibly resenting Dad for sleeping. Sam Matson would be, I knew, asleep.

Dad had taught me almost everything he had learned about wilderness survival. In fact, he'd said once that I ought to hike by myself sometime, to sleep alone in the woods, miles from anyone else or a town.

Well, I thought, here I am. To remind me even further where I was, an owl hooted in an overhead tree. Other than that single sound, the night was quiet. I could have stroked the silence like a sleeping dog.

I'd been grateful, and would continue to be, that Dad had flashed me the green light regarding this trip. Even against Mom's vehement protesting. She wasn't an ardent fan of the great outdoors. Vacations to my mother, who was an English teacher, meant a seashore and not a mountain forest. Plus a hotel room, restaurant dining, and a relaxing bath in a tile tub, among bubbles. Or reading on a beach. Sometimes her private laughter would dance above her head, some unseen pink parasol of pleasure.

I was glad Mom couldn't see me now, she who wanted a writer for a son and not an outdoorsman.

One evening last summer, when Dad was away on business, Mom and I were standing side by side at the kitchen sink, doing the supper dishes together. She'd asked me whether or not I was planning to write something longer than a three-paragraph book report.

"First," I told her, "I've got to tackle a wild adventure, all by myself. Please don't take my head off if I tell you that maybe, just *maybe*, I'm going to attempt the biggest project of my life this coming fall." I handed her a sudsy dinner plate. "It's so big that only the laundry will know how scared I am."

Mom smiled. "What sort of a project?"

"Well, I just might play hooky from school for a week, and maybe go look for Jo Silver."

That was when Mom dropped the plate.

After we'd finished policing up the kitchen, I went upstairs to read, then came downstairs again to grab a brownie and a glass of milk. Mom was sitting in her chair on the sunporch, listening, it appeared, to the evening choir of bugs and frogs. She looked up at me, smiling.

"You have milk on your upper lip," she had said, "but on you, it looks good."

I smiled back, sat in the rocker, and we talked for an hour or more about my future. And somehow we drifted into philosophy and how humanity had evolved. Mom had plenty of ideas to share with me, as always, and we discussed how certain activities began. She told me that perhaps a primitive birdwatcher had observed an oriole constructing the miracle of a hanging nest and the man became a weaver. A hunter had twanged the string of his bow, found it pleasing to his ear, and invented the harp. And maybe someone watched a mudwasp building her home and became a potter.

"I'm lucky," I told her, "to have you for a mother."

Actually, had she been able to see me right now, I thought, cozily curled up in this sleeping bag, under nylon in case of rain, Mom might breathe a bit easier. And then, like my father, drift off to sleep. Yet, come morning, Mom would feel guilty that she'd slept.

It made me grin. Almost laugh. Right about now, I was thinking in the dark, I would rather kiss Mom goodnight than kiss Amy.

Mentally, I'd tucked in both my parents, and wished them slumber, a lullaby to ease *my* mind, not theirs. Dad might have told Mom a bedtime story about how competent I was in the woods. I'll wager it wasn't helping her a great deal. Mom would worry. Tomorrow, at Stamford High where she taught, she probably would be in a half daze all day. A walking zombie.

I rolled over, wondering what time it was and whether or not most of the guys had already crashed the feathers, back at North Academy. Maybe they were all asleep. All except one. A man, I recently discovered, who kept his own copy of *My Sky* in his office. Dr. Abraham Gray, I had a hunch, would be awake right now, wondering where I was. But knowing why.

"Kenny," he'd said, as the two of us sat in his cramped little office two days ago, "this trip of yours could be..."

"Foolhardy."

He nodded. "I know how much both of us admire our favorite writer. And that's good. All boys have to find one author whose work inspires them to venture out into the world and tackle its trouble."

"Great," I said. "That means, sir, you approve of my going to Pine Corners and trying to locate Lost Pond and Jo Silver Fox."

Dr. Gray had scowled and scolded. "You know damn well I *don't* approve. Have you telephoned your parents about this proposed adventure?"

I shifted on the hard chair. "No, but I'm planning on it. Honest, I really will. That's a vow. It wouldn't be right just to split."

"No, it wouldn't. I'm sorry, in a way, you're letting me in on all of this. It places me in an awkward position. Not only with Dean Stockton, but with my own conscience. It's the latter that's nagging me."

"I understand, sir."

"And, I shall mark you absent, even though I'll loathe myself for doing so."

As I hooked up a sneaker to rest on my knee, I said, "Sir, I guess that's only fair. I didn't stop in to get you to cover for me."

"I know you didn't." His voice sounded less harsh, as though his thoughts had taken him away, on a trip of his own. As he talked, the old bachelor's face had somehow lost its usual enthusiastic expression. Instead, the wrinkles over his eyebrows had deepened, as he tore at a hangnail. "You're still a boy. There's so much in life you haven't even begun to enjoy. I don't want you to get yourself killed. Think, for the love of Heaven, what your death or disappearance would mean to your parents."

"I've thought about all of that, sir."

"And?"

"I *have* to go. Because, if I don't, I'll rot here at school and brood about my not going. And then continually cuss my own chicken."

Making a sour face, Dr. Gray grunted. "*Chicken*, eh? That stupid and immature term has crashed more motorbikes, drowned children, tempted more useless dares..."

"I agree. No doubt it really has."

My prof helped himself to a deep breath. "You adolescent lunatic, you're too young to take such a gamble. When people my age die, when I bury dear friends, it's sorrow enough. But when a *child*..."

"I'm not a child. I'm almost seventeen."

He cleared his throat. "I'm sorry. Excuse me, Ken. But please understand that, to *me*, and especially to your mother and father, you're still our beardless baby boy."

"Yeah. I mean *yes sir*, I am."

"Worse yet, I've seen your personal record, Kenneth, and you're an *only* child. You have no brothers, no sisters. Have you *any idea* what it would mean to dear Mr. and Mrs. Matson, if... if..."

He pulled off his glasses.

"Long ago," he said, "I had a...a dear friend, someone so very distant and yet so close. Anyhow, to capsule a long story, this person..."

"Died?"

"Worse. So, remembering your parents, I know what it's like to watch someone lose everything, except life, and then have to live with it. Ken, it's more tragic than death. Believe me."

"I believe you, sir."

"I'm not your father. Alas, I am not *anyone's* father or mother. All I am is a moth-eaten relic, a stone statue in a garden of youth."

Standing up, the tall and lanky teacher turned his back to look out of his tiny window. The tweed suit of brown that he so often wore seemed to sag on his scarecrow body. Both of the jacket's cuffs were frayed and looked tired. Almost defeated. He sat down again, reached for a pipe, stuffed it more with annoyance than with tobacco, and spiked it into his firmly-set mouth.

"I wish you hadn't told me," he said. "And I regret telling you lads never to allow formal education to stunt your growth. That tomfool remark of mine has brought me little but misunderstanding in my so-called *academic* community."

"Okay, but you already have told us. I don't get it. Last year, when I told you about Jo Silver Fox, and *My Sky,* you seemed so pleased, so happy I'd discovered it all."

"Enough," he said. "We've apparently reached a stalemate here. I can see that you're intent on going, with or without the school's permission."

I stood up. "Maybe," I said, "I better get moving. I'm sorry if I upset you, Dr. Gray. Honest."

He didn't answer but stared straight ahead at his messy old bulletin board. I waited, feeling that there was something else that he was compelled to tell me. "You mustn't go," he whispered. "Not alone."

I shook my head. "Wrong. I have to do it, on my own. I'm going to find out if Jo Silver is still alive. And if so, where." I had a fleeting hunch that he somehow ached to go with me. Was he afraid? No, not Abraham Gray. He went to bat for every kid at North, both in the classroom and in Dean Stockton's office. Most of all, he'd level with us. That was old Honest Abe's reputation. "It was you," I said, "who introduced me to Jo Silver's writing. You let me read that article, *Quest for Liberty.* Remember, sir?"

"Oh, yes...I well remember. Damn it."

"Then what's wrong? Last year, you seemed so delighted that I'd figured out that Jo Silver Fox had written *My Sky*, just as you had done."

He looked up at me, biting down on the black stem of a beat-up briar pipe that he had not bothered to light. His hands twisted the book of matches.

"It isn't *your* job to rescue hermits."

"Sir, whose job is it?"

"Not yours. A lad of sixteen shouldn't have to tote such a burden. Someone *else* ought to be going to Lost Pond instead of you."

I shrugged. "Who?"

As I turned over in my sleeping bag, I realized that Dr. Abraham Gray had not answered my last question.

6

I awoke, tasting last night's beans.

Why hadn't I brushed my teeth? It was a minor oversight, yet I didn't want to allow myself to fall into the trap of forgetfulness. I'd have to stick to a steady and trustworthy regimen, a routine. No getting slipshod.

As I moved, my right hip ached a bit. No problem. The night stiffness always came from forest dampness.

Usually, at school, I was the last guy up. Except when my teeth were into something; and at those times, I was often up all night. But such spurts of industry were, perhaps, too rare. I'm lazy. One time, in the science lab, all of the other guys were *standing* at their black counters, constructing our assigned experiment. I was lying on mine. Dr. Gray commented that, at times, I was about as ambitious as convict labor.

Well, I thought, today I'd show him.

Moving again, I was relieved that I'd done a lot so perfectly. Every article I'd brought, except the light rack of my backpack, was in the sleeping bag with me. I had not committed the error of hanging my parka on a tree limb, then having to wear it either rain-soaked or damp with dew. It wasn't quite morning. From somewhere, I guessed quite near, a bluejay shrieked its abrasive call, as though it were an alarm.

Then I heard a human voice!

The early morning was cold, misty, damp, no rustle of leaves by wind which enabled me to smell and hear more. The voice carried, bouncing around the big gray boulders and sifting through the evergreens. As the person had spoken, at once I reasoned that he was not alone. Hearing a second voice, one less shrill, I listened intently. I was correct. There were only two voices, one of which did most of the talking. Almost all.

Its companion merely grunted in response.

I lay almost entirely sheltered under a dead juniper bush, the twisted trunk of which split a nearby rock. Stretching up a hand, I gently shook the juniper, quietly allowing a shower of countless brown needles to sprinkle over my sleeping bag. I reached underneath my bag, withdrew handfuls of pine needles and completed my horizontal mask. Whoever they were, they would have to trip over me in order to discover where I lay.

But I had to pee like crazy.

It was all that spring water that I had, last evening, forced myself to drink. Nerves, I told myself. Keep calm. The two visitors probably knew these woods and trails. I didn't. So my best defense, I figured, was to stay put with my hunting knife in my hand.

"You comin' long, Harley?" the shrill higher-pitched voice was now inquiring. His tone sounded rasping and unpleasant.

"Yeah," said Harley.

"He can't of went too far on a late start. Not up here," Shrill Voice insisted. "The stupid kid's probably lost."

Hearing his distant insult annoyed me. The voices

sounded to be about the length of a football field away from me, a hundred yards or so. Not much closer. The odds that they would somehow stumble up on my camp were, I figured, at least a hundred to one. Maybe more.

"No sweat," I told myself.

The dumbest thing to do would be to spook, to jump up and go crashing through the brush, yelling for help. I wasn't about to do that. Yet, when I heard Shrill Voice again, he was coming closer.

"I ain't waitin' all day," said Shrill Voice, sounding impatient that Harley couldn't, or just wouldn't, keep up.

Harley didn't answer. Instead, I heard a flock of what I guessed to be sparrows suddenly chirp and scold at a morning interruption. Whoever, he was, good old Harley was a lot closer to me than Shrill Voice.

"Harley? You thar? Where ya be?"

"Hush yer mouth," Harley grunted in his slow, almost methodical, tone. He spoke as though his mind had to consider how to pronounce even simple words.

"Find somethin', didja?" asked Shrill.

There was a long pause, then an urgent rustle of branches, as Shrill Voice made his way along the ridge to join his friend. Both men were now closer.

"He come along here way," Harley said.

Another pause. This time much longer. The men were stone quiet. Not hearing them felt worse than over-hearing their every word. But they didn't sound to be moving. I wondered if they could hear my breathing. Try as I might, I couldn't force my lungs to stop panting.

"I didn't hear nothin' at all," said Shrill, his nasal alto twanging out through the mist of dawn.

I didn't welcome any sunlight. Not now. One good thing in my favor was the mountain mist, almost thicker than porridge, which wouldn't burn off much before noon. If I couldn't see more than twenty or thirty feet, neither could they.

"Nothin' but birds," said Shrill.

He was the talker. Harley, the listener. Of the two, I figured it would be the grunting Harley who possibly owned the brain. Shrill Voice was all mouth.

I heard feet, then a heavy and labored puffing. Not moving anything except my eyes, I strained to see beyond the drifting mist. And I finally could make out a burly shadow. It had to be Harley, out of breath, unable to keep up with the scampering Shrill Voice. I heard footsteps and presumed them to have been Shrill's, approaching.

"Hush," warned the former. "Keep silent."

I'd been right. It surely was big beefy Harley. I could hear his breathing and my own. He disappeared. Shrill Voice wasn't about to be quiet. "I don't hear nothin' or nobody. You kin tell your sister, fat old Libby, she's full of..."

The shrill mouth never got to tell Harley Potter what his sister was full of. I heard a sharp slapping sound, as though a big hand had cuffed a skinny face. Shrill Voice yelped.

"Damn ya, Vernon," growled Harley.

Then I heard what I guessed to be a well-targeted *kick*, one that caused the abused Vernon to scream even louder. They moved away and into the fog. Their voices retreated with them, Harley saying little and Vernon griping with each retreating step.

I waited for at least twenty minutes.

Then I crawled out of my bag to quietly hiss my water into the needles and leaves. It felt like Heaven. My bladder couldn't have retained it a second longer. From below the ridge, far away now, I heard the downhill-headed pair, Harley, the bully, and his complaining sidekick.

They were still arguing. Harley's deep voice was now gone. All I could still hear was Vernon's fading, yet unrelenting, whimper, about his lack of money. And no job.

I couldn't eat.

All I could manage to do was pull on my parka, sit on a log, and tremble. My pants felt wet. I must have been more chicken than I thought.

It made me really angry, knowing that I'd heard good old Harley and Vernon possibly arguing over my wallet. Or how to waste me. I sort of wished Mom had talked me out of coming. Why hadn't I listened? All I did, during our telephone chat, was shoot off my own big mouth, endlessly. I hadn't listened to Dr. Gray's warnings either.

Finally I ate my breakfast. A slice of ham plus one more apple. That would be all I'd allow myself. The apple tasted super as it flushed away the overnight hint of beans. I wiped my knife blade on my trousers.

"Let's go," I ordered myself.

Rolling up my bag, securing all duffle and gear, my eyes combed the turf for any telltale item I might foolishly leave behind. Nothing. Poking my finger into soft ground, I made a grave for yesterday's candy wrapper, to be sure, so it wouldn't tumble from the pocket of my parka.

"Onward," I said.

Seeing little, I loaded myself into a human pack mule, consulted my compass, and headed west, into fog. Reason hinted that, with my new compass which I'd purchased from Mr. Clepp, I perhaps would not need a trail. Dad had always told me how keen my nose was at being able to sniff out a lake.

Maybe I was part bloodhound.

Dogs!

How come, I asked myself as I hiked upward, the two men hadn't thought to bring hounds? It was possible they didn't own any. Or, to make another guess, they had no article of my clothing with which to prime a scent. My dry boots on granite or pine needles would leave hardly a trail at all.

"Remember," I whispered to myself, "to keep your boots dry. And watch where you're walking. Every step."

My knife notched another tree. Doing so, I made certain to cut as high as I could reach. The signs, at a constant height and on the uphill side, would be more obvious for me to spot, later on. Far safer from possible pursuit. Coming to a bare boulder that looked invitingly flat to sit on, I jerked my orange pack off my shoulders and rested. Sniffing, I smelled no water. No damp-ground vegetation. Off to my left, something moved. I froze, waiting. It turned out to be a mother raccoon with a pair of kits. Her twins were, I guessed, almost half grown.

As I remained motionless, she looked at me from ten or twelve feet away, her nostrils pumping to inhale information. With her black eyes focusing on me, she stopped, a signal for her kits to stop too.

One did. The other approached me slowly.

The adult made a noise in her throat, warning the curious kit to retreat to her. He wouldn't. Instead, his black nose sniffed the toe of my right boot.

"Boo," I said softly.

Away he ran; so did his parent and the other kit, concluding that I was not, after all, a friend or merely a part of the Adirondack scenery. I rested, and then was totally awed when back all three of them came, still curious, wondering what I was. Perhaps, they decided, I was merely some new larger form of food. Maybe a one hundred and thirty pound crayfish.

According to Dad, the most knowledgeable nimrod I knew, a coon will eat about anything...bugs, fish, nuts, seeds...but what they really enjoy most is a crawdad, a crayfish.

"Hello," I whispered to the coons.

They ran again, but, this time, not nearly as far. Not out of my sight. Only a few paces. Then back again, cautiously, sniffing and blinking, and otherwise looking furry and adorable. If a guy ever gave his girl a baby pet raccoon, she'd love him forever.

I'd like, I was sort of dreaming, to give one to Amy Woodward.

She was a girl I knew, back home in Stamford, Connecticut. Amy was the quiet type. She talked some, and when she did, at least she had sensible stuff to say. Maybe I liked her because she liked books and didn't chew gum.

We didn't go to new movies. Instead, Amy and I watched the really *old* flicks on TV. Hollywood had forgotten how to make a good movie. Instead, they made *special effects*, like something blowing up. Movies at theaters never let you get to *know* anybody. All it was, to me, was just wide-screen Atari.

"Want a crayfish?" I asked the coons.

It hit me! Where would a raccoon family be going to find a crayfish breakfast? Not up here on the high ground.

Only to a *pond*.

7

I stood up.

This time, the three coons really streaked away, a trio of brown blurs. Pulling on my pack, I gave respected chase, pursuing as quietly as I could, remaining mostly unseen. And hoping eventually to be ignored.

Dad always said, "Kenny, you're too eager to be a tracker. Don't try to overtake your quarry. Just tag along. Sooner or later, the two of you will meet up... and *bang!*"

I winced, remembering.

That was my weakness as a hunter. I never actually ached to fire a rifle or a shotgun and kill some animal. Worse yet, to wound or cripple it. At least I had the guts to tell Dad my feelings. "I just don't dig hurting some little critter, even if it's a moose," I told him.

"You track," he'd said, "and I'll fire."

"Okay," I'd said.

As far as I was concerned, the real rush I got from hunting was the pursuit, not the kill. I enjoyed meeting animals, observing, then bidding them a harmless and bloodless farewell. I felt no need, absolutely none, to

prove that I was Big Ken Matson, a hairy-chested gunner of game. And I wasn't going to keep a trophy room
in my home, featuring a wood-panel wall with a lot of
little furry heads on it, with antlers.

"Howdy, sports fans," I said in my forced baritone.
"This is your host, Macho Matson, for TV's newest sport-
ing show, Killer Ken's Korner. Now this head up here,
over my fireplace, is a field mouse. Or *was* a field mouse,
before I wasted him with my trusty Army surplus 155
howitzer. Yeah, boys, there's only one satisfying way to
bag a field mouse. And that's with field artillery."

I fell down laughing.

That's it, Matson, I was thinking. Let your stupid
funnybone take over to ruin it all. I got up, recalling
how I'd cut loose with the comedy at North Academy,
even in class. A lot of the dudes wouldn't even smile.
They'd usually miss the joke. Their one pleasure was
ridicule.

Dr. Abraham Gray always laughed with me, whether
it was in Science or Music. Honest Abe taught both. He
was a real wit. The name of our glee club, thanks to Dr.
Gray, was called the O. K. Chorale.

Wow, I thought, what a super guy old Honest Abe
Gray really is. Always gung ho for any project. Even a
skit.

I laughed again as I walked, trying to keep my three
raccoon friends in distant sight. What tickled me so
much was my memory of the skit that Dr. Gray and I
had acted out, last semester. We did a take-off on a
spaghetti western. He played the female lead, Ava Lava,
in drag; and I played the hero who stood at least a foot
shorter. I was Retardo Molesto. I giggled, remembering. Our skit, a scene from an Italian movie, we called
"Wagon Tongue," the saga of a cowardly cowboy and
an eager gal. We purposely fluffed a lot of our romantic

lines, and then we'd say, "Oh *skit!*"

It was a real hoot.

Even a few of the nerds laughed, and old Dr. Gray cackled louder than anyone else, except for me. I broke up. Honest Abe Gray is about six feet four, leaner than Ichabod Crane; so a physique like his just couldn't handle two Persian melons. He sure made a hot Ava Lava, wearing lipstick on his hornrim face that looked as though he'd applied it with a trowel.

But, for some strange reason, Dr. Gray had opposed my solitary search for Jo Silver. Had he wanted to come with me? I wondered why.

Hiking on, I came to a clearing which featured an old dead apple tree. No one, surely, had planted it up here on a mountain. Yet here it had grown, perhaps as a result of a bird having eaten a seed which fell here in its droppings. Looking up, I spotted a bird's nest, now abandoned, which had held, I presumed, youth upon the gray shoulder of age. I wondered if the old apple tree had enjoyed the twitterings of his bird grandchildren.

When I saw the fox, I stopped.

There he lay, paws forward and ears up, on a large rock, twenty feet above my head, looking down at me with his intelligent eyes. Deciding I was a boring subject and far too big for breakfast, he yawned. Then, without pardon, he got to his feet, stretched like a cat, and trotted from sight. The last I saw of the fox was his red tail, a departing plume, straight up.

Ahead, the coons were still dancing along, the kits following Mama wherever she went. Her two shadows. "Lady Coon," I said rather quietly, "I hope you're in the mood for crayfish so avidly that nothing else will do."

I followed my coon trio, realizing that I had no idea

now where I was. My knife hadn't notched a tree in at least a half hour. So I nicked one, for insurance. Then another a few yards later. Ahead of me, I heard a buzzing sound. Breaking into a lazy trot, I caught up to the three raccoons. Mama was high in a tree, pawing a hole, and sending down hunks of something which hit the leafy earth and stuck.

Honey.

It was a super sight to see. Too unreal to be believed. The kits were attacking the bee honey as though they hadn't eaten for a month. Bees flew everywhere so I retreated to a respectful distance, shaking my head, wondering if I was the first woodsman to ever witness such a circus.

"I'll be kinked," I said.

Previously, I'd always assumed that only bears went after a beehive, to rob it. I had been dead wrong. Then I remembered. Dad told me that an old Huron Indian that he'd met, years and years ago, had called a raccoon *the little brother of the bear.*

I could hardly wait to tell Dr. Gray and Dad about the coons and the bee tree. And to tell Jo Silver Fox if I got lucky.

I moved closer to watch.

The coons were having themselves a risky picnic, licking everything in sight, while the bees were merely having a fit. The coons got stung. Every second or two, one of them would flinch, or yelp like a human baby. But they didn't desert their sweet feast. Watching, I tried to convert my brain into a camera, to record it all for Dr. Gray to see, later on. Yet I guessed there would be other information he'd want more, despite his warning me not to go.

The truth about Jo Silver, someone who held a special meaning for him, and I couldn't quite understand why.

I felt that there was something inside Dr. Gray which he didn't tell me.

Other than Mom and Dad, Dr. Gray was the only person on earth who knew where I was headed and why. I sighed, recalling my folly in Pine Corners. Wrong, you jerkhead, I told myself. Mr. Clepp knows. So does the charming groceress, Libby Potter. Add to that those two swell guys, basso Harley and whining Vernon. I tried to laugh at my stupidity. Yet I couldn't honestly smile. Maybe by this time, half the citizenry of Pine Corners knew and figured to be somehow dealt in.

It would have saved time and telephoning for everyone if I'd simply placed an advertisement in the local weekly newspaper. If they had one. *The Pine Corners Bugle* maybe. The ad could have said:

> Sixteen-year-old moron hits town, searching for Lost Pond, seeks Jo Silver Fox. Carries cash aplenty and appears to be a born victim. For manhunt details, please contact Harley or Vernon.

Grabbing a young pine for support, I giggled myself silly. But it felt so super. Matson, I thought, you're really a spaz. You've flipped, kid. You possibly blew it. Lost or shot, you'll wind up wasted.

"Easy," I said.

Kenny Matson, *me,* is the only friend I've got up here, so perhaps I'd better throttle down. Slap my gears into low and take stock.

The raccoons had apparently licked themselves to the gastric brim with bee honey and now were waddling off. I crept forward. At the first truculent sting, I intended to reverse my charge and chicken out. Reaching down, I picked up a gooey comb, tasted it, and spat out some wax. It took several spits. The honey wasn't bad. Good, in fact. But as my three raccoon friends had made rather a mess at my feet, there wasn't much honey left that was free of leaves or grit.

I heard a loon!

The bird's haunting cry was a long and slender type of noise, fluttering and unmistakable. A stiletto of sound that pierced the mist almost into a wounded and bleeding echo. Water, I thought. Like a duck, a loon is a lake creature and its sound, even though a long way off, made me smirk.

"Matson," I said, "you're on target."

I didn't know where I was; and in a sense, that pleased me too. In an idiotic way. Simple, I thought. A guy just has to get *lost* before he can find Lost Pond. Checking the compass, I noted how little the needle told me and wondered again if Mr. Clepp had been accurate. No doubt any dominant presence of iron ore could affect the accuracy of a compass to the point of rendering it totally useless. From now on, I'd consult the sun.

Again I heard the loon.

Its lonely note did not seem to come from any single direction. The thin cry merely hung in the air, as though part of the mist, one of many instruments within the music of a mountain morning.

So I hiked due west.

8

"Now *think*, Matson," I told myself.

The raccoons had quietly disappeared. Into a hole, I presumed, in which they would sleep away the day. The honey had been their bedtime snack.

Ahead, the boulders became larger and higher. All granite, and Yankee stubborn in Puritan gray. Two, in particular, appeared to be twin granite castles, as though they housed some giant mountain king and his queen. I had to cut north, for what I estimated to be over a mile, intending to skirt the shorter of the two castles. Touching the gray rock dampened my hand. Somewhere, beyond or inside this massive hunk of granite, was moisture. A lot of it.

Lost Pond?

There was a gap between the two huge castles of rock. So I climbed, higher and higher until the muscles of my legs screamed to each other what a fool I was. My pack felt heavier than a boulder.

The enormous rock proved rather simple to climb, in terms of route, not steepness. It was almost straight up. Yet its rugged face was pocked by hundreds of ledges, some of which were lathered in green moss and whiskered by dry sprouts of juniper. The juniper berries were, I knew, not what any civilized tongue would welcome as a gourmet's treat. Yet they were food. And *free!* No charge by Libby Potter.

Halfway up to the gap, I rested on a damp ledge, shedding my burdensome pack. All I did for a full two minutes was puff, pant, and chew up more juniper berries.

"Not bad," I told the berry in my mouth. I'd heard that distillers used juniper berries to blend gin. So, I concluded as I chewed, a martini was little more than berries and a vermouth grape. Maybe, I thought, I'll become drunk. The notion of becoming high, this high up, almost prodded me to spit out a blue juniper berry. But instead, I swallowed it. "Yum," I said, to convince myself that I was really partying up here.

To my left, the gray rock had become almost black and shiny, from wetness. Some strong force was pressuring the water through tiny cracks in the granite. Being thirsty, I licked the wet grainy rock. It made me remember what Dr. Gray had lectured us, last year in Physics class, about pumps.

"A pump," he had said, "works on a simple theory. Air can be compressed. Water cannot."

But, I reasoned as my tongue lapped at the wet granite, certainly no air was being compressed up here. Nobody was pumping. What else could force the water through a stone? Another form of pressure, some natural pump, perhaps.

The answer came. More water!

"That's what hurts your ears when you dive down as far as you can endure. It's *water pressure*," Dr. Gray had told us.

I looked up.

"Okay," I asked, "what do I do now?"

Perhaps, I guessed, a lot of the local folks, like good old Harley and Vernon, had never bothered to wonder about the theory of what pumped what. Water, to them, was merely there. Available, to cook with, for drinks, and, possibly with the exception of the fragrant Libby Potter, to use for washing and bathing. I laughed, musing if Miss Bessie Quill, she of professional fame, smelled anything like Libby.

I'd kissed Amy Woodward once.

Just one time, last month. It was mid-September, and she was leaving Stamford to go to Mount Holyoke College. Amy was in her first year. I was grateful, I thought, that Amy Woodward was so short, because she was almost eighteen, a year older than I was. She'd be impressed if I found Jo Silver. This, I confessed, was one of my key reasons for this expedition. To impress Amy, to show her I wasn't too young, and to prove that I was as big as all those college guys.

I liked at least a hundred things about Amy. For one, she played the flute and really well. Her idol was Herbie Mann, a flute pro.

My legs still ached.

So, I figured, I'd just hunker here on the ledge, on soft moss, and loaf for a bit. Another five minutes to think about Amy. To my mind, she sure was a whistler of a girl. Love, I mused, might be a form of insanity, yet it was a nifty way to go nuts.

Sundrops spiked down, like rain, blossoming specks of wild mustard still prospering in the autumn. The day was brightening. A soft golden advance of late morning sun was starting to warm my right cheek. Air touched my ear with a shy whisper. I felt good. It was pleasing to know that, as I sat on the ledge with my back to granite, I was facing the east. A super feeling, just to relax and moondog about Amy Woodward.

She was the only girl that I could talk to, face to face, and not mumble idiotic things. Plus the even stranger fact that when we were together, I didn't trip, or drop my books, or all of the other turkey acts I performed around most girls. Even when they were a year or two younger than I was, they still didn't ignite or beknight me into any semblance of princely grace.

A day or so later, after our first clumsy and experimental kiss, I stopped at Mount Holyoke, on my way north to Lake Placid and school, to see her. I stayed overnight there. On the floor.

I had not, I recalled, been totally honest with Amy Woodward.

Oh, it was true enough that I wanted to see *her* again. But there was also another reason to visit her college. Jo Silver Fox was, I had known, a graduate of Mount Holyoke. Which meant that I could go to their library, drag Amy with me, and do some research.

Being with Amy, I'd thought as the two of us strolled her campus, and also being able to excavate a few facts about Jo Silver, really doubled my pleasure. It reminded me of a passage in *My Sky*. "A key coincidence can unlock the mystery of every life," the book had said. True enough, because both Amy Woodward and Jo Silver had chosen Mount Holyoke. That in itself was one heck of a coincidence.

We went into the basement of a college building which Amy called, for some reason, Wilbur.

There, in the archives, Jo Silver Fox's picture was in an old yearbook. She had been the valedictorian of her class. Yet I hadn't been at all surprised. Jo Silver had been, in later years, much more. A botanist, zoologist, musician, poet, nature writer, and had won the National

Rifle Award, for women, as a sharpshooter. Two years later, Jo Silver Fox had attended Yale Divinity School, graduating with honors. That was all. Her brief biography ended.

During the summer, I had loaned Jo Silver's book *My Sky*, to Amy. We discussed it over sodas, pizza, and beach sand on the Connecticut shore. And more, it had been Amy Woodward who had almost goosed me into my decision to find Lost Pond and to meet the woman I so revered but had never met.

"Thanks, Amy Woodward," I said. Although I only said it once, her name kept ringing like a nobody-home telephone.

The two of us found something else in the archives at Mount Holyoke College. Not only yearbook pictures. Some social pictures as well. Photos of college kids at parties and dances. Only one of Jo Silver. She was holding hands with a boy whose hair had been parted in the middle.

The rock I was sitting on was commencing to nag, yet I didn't even fake getting to my feet. All I wanted to do was sit there and savor what an exciting year I'd enjoyed. In so many different ways. Someday, I knew, Amy Woodward would gradually become the most important person in my entire life. But as for right now, on this coppery Adirondack day, finding the lady who had written *My Sky* was my only mission.

In the yearbook, at Mount Holyoke College, her picture had been beautiful. Jo Silver Fox looked like any American college girl of the times. She had short raven hair, cut in a feathery style, and almost burning eyes, even in a black and white photograph.

Other than complexion, I'd seen no outward sign, or emblem, of her Indian blood. Her father, John Silver Fox, I already knew, had been a full-blooded Mohawk guide, a man who had married a white woman. Their one child, a daughter, had been named Johanah.

I sighed. "I guess they called her Jo."

There was so little I really knew, or understood. Why had Jo Silver disappeared? And even harder to ponder was why a man like my favorite prof, Dr. Honest Abe Gray, had so opposed my search. I was glad for his concern.

Yet he had known that it was sort of my destiny to try. I told him it was.

I'd never believed in destiny or coincidence a whole lot, at least not until I'd read *My Sky* a couple of times. Even now, I wasn't a rabid enthusiast. But the book had said that each man, each woman, and every creature on Earth has a key to its own spiritual kingdom. The key hangs on a cord, a lanyard around one's neck perhaps, to thump upon a heart. The cord was a rainbow to span twin clouds.

Thinking about *My Sky* made me wonder whether or not I had a key. If so, I was about to fit it into a now-empty keyhole, turn my key, and crack open a very mysterious door.

At a place called Lost Pond, with an old woman who somehow was calling me to find her.

9

I climbed higher.

It was really tough going. My hand was bleeding from where I'd carved it against the sawtooth edge of a cracked rock. I guessed what had cracked it. Ice. A water pocket, made by a winter thaw which was then followed by a quick freeze. The water froze and expanding ice had split the granite.

"Nature," the author of *My Sky* had written, "is the only truth. Much of the rest is human invention, prefabrication, and ego."

I looked around me. Here I was, alone, and therefore surrounded by all of Nature and none of humanity. God and Kenny Matson. Wow, I thought, what a team! It was a clean feeling, beyond soapy. I whipped my bloody hand in rapid circles in order to flush it clean. The bleeding finally stopped, formed a scab, and I could see the trickled blood on my palm had browned to dryness. Most of it wore off as I climbed.

The osprey almost stopped my heart!

Even after it exploded from a crack in the granite,

above my head, I didn't realize at once what it was. Not even a bird. As I almost flinched backwards and fell to my death, I saw my mother's face. Not my father's, only hers, and she was screaming.

Then, clinging tightly to the granite shards, I imagined my own broken body, far below, lying in a twisted and lifeless ragdoll pose.

"Bug-off!"

Looking up, I saw the circling osprey.

Goshawk, I'd first guessed. But then the dramatic curl of the wingtips easily identified the osprey. There was little time to waste on admiration. If its nest was above me, I wasn't about to commit suicide, by talon, and trespass anywhere near it. As I climbed around the area, avoiding it by a good forty feet, I listened again and again to the osprey's irate scream.

"Bug-off! Bug-off! Bug-off!" it seemed to be screeching at my rude intrusion.

Edging away from danger's nest, I smiled at the circling, scolding bird. I was almost joyously intoxicated that it was an osprey. Most of them, that I'd seen in the past, nested at the top of a dead tree that stood in water. All, in fact.

An osprey meant one thing.

A pond.

The thought made me giddy with its foolishness. How, I asked myself, if I see a pond, will I know which one it is? There won't be a label. You're not on a map, Kenny. Mother Nature hardly hangs out a shingle that says WELCOME TO LOST POND. Hands sweating, but mouth eagerly dry, I climbed upward over the rough granite faster than a spooked spider.

The pack now weighed ounces, or a gram. My heart was even lighter.

Carelessly, my right boot dislodged a basketball-sized

stone; it bounced downward and ended in a brushy crash, far below. Watching it fall caused me to swallow the empty nothing of fear in my throat. Until now, I hadn't bothered too much with downward glances. I was higher than I'd realized. Jerking out my compass, I read its confused needle. East, it said. Lode? "How much iron ore could be up here?" I asked the compass. Some, it answered. The fluttering needle was lost too. Pocketing my now useless compass, I climbed more granite stairs, counting each ledge for some nonexistent reason.

One... two... three...

I scaled up to thirteen and reached the crotch, the gap between the king's castle and the queen's. Here, the granite wall evened out gradually to become a floor; and I stood freely, hands in the air, a flea's mite below and between the pair of peaks.

As I ran along the rolling plateau of granite, my boots leaping over crevices, I whipped my head in all directions. No water. Wrong, I told myself. An osprey doesn't roost in a desert. Had I misread its silhouette against the sky? And, I asked myself, had it instead been merely a mountain hawk? I stopped, positive that I had heard a reply, an answer to the question I was posing. Then I did hear, clearly, sharply, and happily.

Again I heard a loon.

Its toot was long, lonesome, like a final whistle to a quitting-time mill. The note was reedy, watery. Wet.

Closing my eyes, I let my nose inhale my share of a high mountain breeze. A wilderness fragrance of nothing, yet everything, containing a wisp of every spice on Nature's lofty shelf. Keep your eyes closed, Kenny Matson, I ordered myself, and smell. Right now. I smelled it. Mud, dead fish, beaver or muskrat dung, ferns, the rotty remains of freshwater mussels and mountain pond snails. And wet wood, the smell that only a fallen log emits, when it lies fallow, half-covered by water.

"Yahoo," I whispered.

Then I said it again, and repeated it somewhat louder, finally yelling it up into a noon sky to a supreme sun. "Yahoo! It's here. Yaaahooooo!"

I felt groggy, the granite king's fool, standing on a table of gray rock, listening to my last *yahoo* echo and echo, bounding away to a faded Adirondack silence.

Looking up into the blue, I said "Thank you," to an open sky.

The sun told me how to march west. Heeding its truth, I marched, pranced, danced, and skipped my way along the flattening granite that upon occasion became quite bumpy with lesser boulders. I was an ant, scampering across a gray placemat set on a table between a queen and king.

I came to one expansive patch of high juniper. No berries. The trunks of these very low trees had all been mercilessly twisted by the cruel fingers of winter's wind. They were matted by ferocity; tangled, woven, ripped, and then somehow knitted again into a pattern fit only to shawl a peak. Or a rough patch on a granite monarch's knee.

Hearing a distant cry, I squinted upward to the sun, rewarded with what could only have been a golden eagle, just a speck, however, a russet jewel that glided from the crown of king to queen. A sky sperm, one soaring prince of gold, creasing the sunshine light, uniting royalty, and slashing Heaven into two equal shares. My neck ached from the strain of looking at the sky. Yet it was healthy hurting. People don't see a golden eagle very often. Some never shall. He was my first. Seeing the eagle disappear, beyond clouds, I began to wonder what I'd grow up to become. Inside, I sort of wanted to be a writer who would be married to a flutist. Amy Woodward, to be exact.

Loon, osprey, plus the aroma...it all had to tally to one conclusion. My map was correct. A pond was here somewhere.

But where?

Certainly not up here on these rocks. Yet, as I moved along with the straps of my orange backpack starting to impress the meat of my shoulders, I knew I was getting warm. Sweaty, in fact. My hand unzipped my parka.

Sun-oriented, I walked west, remaining atop my newfound land of granite shelf. Gradually, the rock began to slope away to the west and I was hiking downhill. Hearing a loon once more, now much closer, boosted my anticipation. No wonder some confused naturalist or cartographer had named the place Lost Pond.

It really was *lost*.

To be found, perhaps by lucky old Kenny Matson, I thought. My left boot was starting to crimp my instep, so I stopped long enough to loosen the laces. This far from the civility of Pine Corners, if one could call it that, I couldn't afford to hatch a blister. Dad wasn't along to watch me or to nag. Not that my father was overly pesky. He wasn't. However, at times he'd mother-hen me some, especially concerning any minor matter of survival, such as a potential limp.

He'd made me a woodsman.

"Thank you, Pa," I said as I retied my looser boot. A lot of what he'd warned me about was beginning to jell into solid reason.

The grand total of his training was merely this. Alone, I could hack it and survive on my own in a wilderness, without, may I add, reverting to some vulnerable panic or phobia. Dad never really talked about *manhood* a whole lot. He just practiced it, allowing me to taste with my eyes, ears, and nose.

"Survival," Dad once had told me, "is merely a spate of unimportant details that add up to a man's total worth." He had smiled at me. "In a way, Kenny, it's just plain housekeeping. Tending the cathedral of mind, body, and soul."

Thinking about Dad made me bend a grin. I felt the pull of my face muscles, in jest. Sam Matson wasn't a poet. Mom was, but not Dad.

He sold real estate.

10

"Nifty," I said.

The reason I said it was because, ahead of me, the rocks began to thin out, being replaced by trees.

Most of them were pines, plus a tall, spire-like tamarack, looking slim and stately, as though shorn from the front of some forest chapel. There were no hardwoods. Everywhere I looked, conifers: cone-bearing spruces, hemlocks, pines. No autumn foliage of reds, oranges, or yellows, the shades so obviously prevalent back in Pine Corners, despite its name.

The pond smell grew slightly stronger.

Lost Pond *had* to be here. Mainly, because it couldn't have chosen a more obscure place to hide. No hunter, back where I had slept last night, would have bothered to look up and then climb so much stubborn granite. And, from all I'd observed in the past, most hunters were not boys like me. They were mature men, old enough to bankroll an expensive deer rifle, gear, possibly a guide. Hunters were men who had logged enough time at a job to warrant a paid vacation, a situation that would weed out younger males. Unless they had dads like Dad and moms like Mom who'd allow them to shadow along.

Thus, I concluded, middle-aged men and their bulging bellies would *not* be climbing up to where I'd just been standing to watch an eagle. No, not they. Plus, I would wager, local people didn't consult maps.

Lost Pond, therefore, was geographically a well-kept secret. It made me grin, my thought. So well-kept that I couldn't solve it.

"But it's got to be here," I said aloud.

My back ached.

So I pulled off my pack and rested, eating boiled ham, crushed bread, no beans, and an apple. I made sure to eat the apple last so its juices would balance the thirst from the ham.

A red squirrel came to investigate me, possibly to learn why I was here and who or what I was. Finishing the apple, I tossed him the core sac which was rife with seeds. My father had told me about red squirrels. "Anywhere they live," he had said, "they'll drive away the grays. Bitter enemies." I recalled how Dad had said that a red squirrel would actually bite and castrate a male gray. The reds were smaller than the grays, yet far more aggressive.

Looking at the red squirrel, I said, "Wow. You don't fool around, do you? You're in this struggle for keeps."

The remembrance came to me like a soft tap on my shoulder. Something I'd read in *My Sky*, Jo Silver Fox's book. "Survival," she had written, "is a form of morality. *Thou shalt not steal* does not apply, for a strong gull will snatch a fish from the beak of a weaker gull, and that...pardon me, Moses...is obviously our God's unspoken purpose."

The thought pleased me.

"I worship you, Jo Silver," I said. "And I'm going to find Lost Pond, and you, if it takes every Milky Way at Libby Potter's grocery. Even if it requires my standing up to Harley Potter and blessed old Vernon."

I laughed.

Kenny, I thought, you're sounding mighty cocky when those two goons aren't around to challenge you. But this morning you were cringing in your sleeping bag and irrigating your Fruit of the Looms. I had to sneer at my own bravado.

As I continued west, the land sloped into timber instead of granite. Greens and browns replaced the gray rock. And, at last, it felt refreshing to be hiking *downhill* for a change. The pond smell was stronger, more insistent, as if its aroma was urging itself to shout its beckoning bait into my nose. I broke into a trot. But after a brisk two-hundred-yard sprint, my legs started to hurt again.

"Pace yourself, Matson," I panted.

It took all the will power that I could muster to force myself to sit on a fallen log, whip off my pack, and just try to recoup my wind and strength. I'd been stupid to run and risk spraining an ankle. This grassy, weedy place would be a good spot for resting.

Sunlight sprinkled down on me through the high cover of evergreen. About ten feet away, on the north side of a thick spruce, grew arrowroot. Without having to move, I stretched out my hand to pluck a wintergreen leaf. It was a tiny green football-shaped treat, about an inch long. I popped it into my mouth and bit down hard. At first, its flavor was crisply resistant, but finally, after a few more chomps, the wintergreen flavor flooded my mouth with its clean, rewarding taste.

More javelins of sunlight darted down through the high pines, and a soft mountain breeze was carding the resolute grass as though it was a giant pelt of green fur. The pines weren't as thick here. Earlier, I'd passed through a pine forest where the trees were so tightly grouped that the bed of needles bounced beneath my boots. Back there, I'd seen no squirrels and heard no birds. And I had been the only animate object, a human louse, flitting between the toes of silent green giants, the pine patriarchs. It had been a place desolate enough to make even the Lord feel lonesome.

"I'd like to live here," I said, "with Amy."

Perhaps, if my life continued to go well, someday the two of us could be shopping for a home. And some real estate hustler, like Dad, would be showing us houses.

What I loved most about Sam Matson, my father, was his ability to laugh at himself. The doctors, lawyers, and clergymen that I knew in Stamford rarely admitted that they were in the medical, legal, or religious game. Not my dad. To him, his job wasn't some self-annointed *profession.*

Sam was in the real estate *game.*

One evening last summer, after he'd poured an extra scotch, the two of us stayed up late, just to talk and swap lies. Dad really opened up. "Kenny," he said, "there's a healthy pinch of *con* in any line of work."

In fun, I had purposefully widened my eyes at him, feigning youth and innocence. "Certainly not in *real estate,*" I'd said.

Dad sipped his scotch and chuckled. "So much so that, at times, if I want a real laugh, I read my own ads in the *Stamford Advocate.*"

"For example," I said, leading Dad on.

"One house I'm currently peddling has faulty plumbing and exposed wires. So I described it, in our ad, as *quaint.* The dining room, right off the kitchen, is so tiny it wouldn't seat a family of mice. So I called it a *breakfast nook."*

Laughing, I'd told him that I had read the ad too. "What exactly does a *gardener's delight* mean?"

Dad smirked. "It means the place is so overgrown that, to reach the front door, you'd need Tarzan's machete."

It doubled me over. Dad unwrapped a fresh cigar, bit off the end, licked it, and lit up. *"High school convenient,"* Dad continued, "means that every morning *and* afternoon, your front lawn is a drag strip."

I slapped my leg. "How about *sunlit lot?"*

"Oh," said Dad, "that means there's not even one tree on the entire property that's over a foot tall."

"How about the zinger you wrote last week? You remember, it said...*your own babbling brook and wading pool."*

"That," Dad told me, "is merely a realtor's way of not telling you that the basement's flooded."

My stomach hurt. Knees up, slouching into the den chair, I was holding my guts and begging Dad to stop.

He sipped the scotch slowly. "Son, to scratch up a buck in the real estate game, you also have to understand how to name *areas,* as well as define houses."

"Like how?"

"Well, you simply name the development after the particular element of Nature that you totally destroy. If the developer slaughters all the trees, it's Sherwood Forest. Bulldoze away all the hills and it's Powderhorn Heights."

"Nifty."

My father took a puff of his cigar. "Believe me, son, I've sold a fishing shanty to a family of seven. They also had three dogs, two cats, goldfish, and at least five bicycles. If a house is really tiny, your listing reads...*oversized garage."*

"Uncle," I said through my tears. "My ribs can't take any more. Honest."

Dad grinned at me. "Honesty," he said, "has little to do with it. If the shack's overpriced, all you say is *executive*. It'll hook 'em every time."

Hearing him explain it was better than any TV sitcom. Mainly, because it flirted with truth. And also, on the other hand, because I was just now beginning to realize how hard he worked. Rarely did he take a Saturday or Sunday off. He was showing houses days and evenings.

"The biggest sucker of all," Dad said, "is the guy with lots of college education, some Ivy League Wasp. They're easy to spot. Their names are usually backwards."

"What do you mean, backwards?"

"Oh, like Aldridge Henry, or Archer Corliss. I met a new prospect last week whose name is Henderson John." Dad cracked up. "I kid ya not. That is actually this gink's name."

"Did you sell him a house?"

Dad nodded. "Worst klunker on the market. A real dog. Leaky roof, rotten floorboards. I didn't let Mr. John near the upstairs john, because when you flush it, the tank thinks it's a drum and bugle corps, on the Titanic. The house is listed as *executive handyman's dream*."

Rolling off my chair, I flopped around on the oval hooked rug of our den. I was laughing so hard that even my hair hurt.

"Gourmet kitchen," Dad said, "means no microwave."

Sam Matson flicked an ash from the tip of his shrinking cigar. It missed the ashtray and I heard him mutter a colorful word. As I sat on the floor, looking up at him, Dad probably had no idea how much I admired him for his unique brand of honesty. And also why Mom loved him so much.

Dad sighed. "A corps of U. S. Army engineers would need a lifetime to fix that house into being livable. And here's the real topper. You'd never guess what Mr. John does to earn his bread."

"I give up," I said. "Hit me with it."

"He works on Madison Avenue in New York City. He's some sort of a magazine editor."

I asked, "What's the magazine?"

"Good Gracious Living."

11

A fox barked.

Hearing its yap-yap jolted me back from remembering home and the pleasant evening with Dad, to where I was. From a further distance, another fox barked a reply.

"Time to move," I said.

As I shouldered my pack, it felt heavier, the straps feeling sharper as they knifed into my chest muscles. Maybe, I thought, I'd been a bit careless in bringing my beat-up copy of *My Sky* along. Yet I had packed it out of loyalty.

I searched for a trail. Nothing. No signs of humanity. Not a beer can or a crushed cigarette pack. This place was absolute Adirondack virginity, a valley of no dolls, no guys. Being here, I was thinking, was like sneaking into someone else's church. A privacy invasion. The fragrant stillness filled my lungs as I walked, causing me to feel that such a locale would be one of the few places on earth where a woman such as Jo Silver would choose to live.

Alone?

The idea halted my boots. Maybe she was married, or had children, now grown. Or she was living with some mountain man who served, among other capacities, as her personal guardian. Would he shoot me on sight?

My neck itched.

Reaching back, I tried to wedge a hand in front of the top of my backpack, to scratch. The itch turned me around where I stood, with an urge to look behind me. The feeling persisted, the itch, an inkling that I was being observed by someone. Or by something. If not actually watched, somehow the somebody knew or felt my presence. It was more of an uneasy feeling than my experience of early this morning, hearing Harley and Vernon. I had presumed who they were, in almost no time, where they were from as well as that which they sought. Me.

Dad used to joke about the lifestyle of a few mountain characters he knew. "They don't call it *murder* in the Adirondacks," he'd said. "They call it a *hunting accident.*"

"Steady," I told myself.

I stood, turning, sweeping all directions with my eyes, ears, and nose. With good old Harley and Vernon, I had the advantage. That being, that silent Harley was cursed with the pox of his ever-whining pal. Vernon, I decided, was my perfect warning device. A walking burglar alarm.

As I moved on, the ground continued to slope gently downward. The trees here were, I had observed, all pines. So where I walked was an endless fawn carpet of needles. Mostly shade.

I saw one sunny spot.

Grass and weeds joyously grew in its circle, high-lighted by a late-blooming stand of black-eyed Susans.

Yellow petals, long and delicate, with not a black eye but a brown one at the hub. It was October, far too late for daisies or most meadow flowers this far north. Yet not for these Susans.

"Hi," I whispered to them.

Uncanny though it may seem I felt the presence of Jo Silver Fox. The flowers, as I hiked by them, almost faced me to holler her name.

I heard a loon trumpet his tinny horn.

Hot damn, I was thinking. The loon's cry came from dead ahead. I was positive of this. *Do not run*, I repeatedly warned myself as I put spurs to my gait. *Walk!* Only idiots run when they're alone in a wilderness.

Straight ahead, beyond the tree tops, the pine forest seemed less shadowy, lighter, thinner. There had to be open space, a clearing. A pond? It certainly wasn't a baseball field or some airport. Not a public park. I trotted a few steps, carelessly, trying to swallow my throat's mounting tightness. It made me wonder if one could choke on anticipation. I hurried along through a second small clearing of sunlight. Then, a third, which was bigger. More sunny patches came to me as I moved to them, almost in welcome.

Then it happened.

As I hopped over a low clump of brush, the bull-roar wings of a ruffed grouse, a partridge, exploded up from my feet and nearly unglued my sanity. I was not aware that I had yelled until I heard the echo of my idiocy dying somewhere, off among pines.

The grouse soared away, the great fan of her tail showing me brown, white, and then nothing. My entire body sweated wet.

In less than a second I had turned myself into a panting puddle. As my lungs worked, or rather overworked, to catch my wind, my mouth gradually closed and my nostrils took over. Inhaling, I again sensed the strong and pungent smell of lakeshore vegetation. Unmistakable. I walked forward, passing not too near a flat rock where a five-foot rattlesnake lay curled in sunshine, storing itself heat for a chilly October evening that soon would come.

The candle of this day was burning shorter.

Not having brought my watch, for fear of losing or breaking it, I didn't exactly know the time. Up here, there were no classes to get to, nor a bus to catch. And no lights-out hours as there were back at North Academy. Yet, I knew, the rules of a wilderness are indeed far more rigid. Mom, not Dad, had told me this; I could hear her voice telling me again, and it made me want to hug her. Or only to yell out, "Mom...I'm home," and hear her answer. And I wanted to hear her speak my name.

Yanking out my hunting knife, I notched a few thick trunks of pines, cursing myself, because I had forgotten to do it for almost the entire afternoon.

I had also forgotten to eat lunch.

Prying into my backpack was impossible without shedding it, so I didn't feel like bothering. Not at first. Then my reason told me: *Don't rush it.* So I unsaddled myself, selected a huge hunk of compressed bread, reloaded, and continued straight ahead.

I still sweated. Flushing the partridge had really flushed my every pore. But I had to feel grateful. I could have, instead, easily hopped over the brush and stomped on a rattlesnake. My boots would have saved me, however. A rattler rarely strikes high. They are lowball hitters, Dad had said in baseball terms, because most of their prey scurries along the ground. Rattlers aren't dogs. They don't run along a beach, leap into the air, and snap at a frisbee.

I spotted a bright layer of silver. Through the trees, the pond's sparkling surface was one long streak, sliced into segments by pine trunks that stood, as sentries, between the pond and me.

"Easy," I told myself as I rushed forward. All it is is *a* pond. You don't know which one. There won't be a sign or an information booth, no smiling attendant to direct the straying tourist. No one to accost and inquire, "Pardon me, but do you have a color brochure on Lost Pond?"

I wanted to laugh out loud. For several reasons. Because my own humor so tickled me, and because I was now confidently walking to a lost pond, now found. Add to that a third reason. I was going to find Jo Silver!

Reaching the pond, I stopped.

I'd seen mountain ponds and lakes by the score. Yet none of them could match this one, for had God placed water into His own giant baptismal font, here it was. To top it all off, I finally spotted my beckoning loon. I saw his black outline paddle into a stand of tan cattails and disappear. The spreading V of his wake seemed to become bored with itself and softly melted away into the placid water. Hearing a very faint congregation of honks, I looked up to see a trail of dots, high up, across the sky. Canada Geese flying south. More southeast, possibly to pick up Lake Champlain and then to follow the Hudson River route, due south.

I waved to the geese.

As I moved, a large cowfrog dislodged herself from the mud, hopping into the pond water with a *thunk*.

Near the mud where the frog had been, I saw hoofprints, made by deer. They were sharply pointed at both toes, the rear halves slightly separated. It had to be deer. There were, I was sure, no antelope or elk in the Adirondack area. At least, neither Dad nor I had ever seen any. We'd never seen any moose either.

Looking along the shore of the pond, I saw an open grassy area. Much of the grass was still green and was infested with a variety of broadleaf weeds, shorter than the grass, growing very close to the rich, almost black, soil. I stepped closer for some reason, perhaps to find what I then saw. There was a low tunnel through the base of the grasses, about the diameter of a softball or a grapefruit.

"Rabbit," I said.

Stooping, I discovered one tiny item that interested me far more than anything else I'd heard, seen, or smelled. A loop of what appeared to be twisted bark had been set at the tunnel's mouth.

A snare!

I held my breath and my excitement. A hunter had set that snare to catch a rabbit. Some human hand had braided the slender strand of bark into twine. The snare was a sign, more than merely that, a signature.

To me, it said Jo Silver.

12

Click!

The tiny but sharply-honed noise almost pierced my hearing and my fear.

I'd heard a sound such as that a hundred times. Possibly more. There was only one noise like it. And it had come from human hands suddenly clicking together a broken shotgun. Breaking *open* a gun creates little or no noise. But, after a fresh shell is installed into the firing chamber, the prepared click creates a distinct and dangerous warning.

I had an urge to escape.

No, I ordered my courage. Don't panic! *It's time to gamble.* You haven't hiked this far to blow it all with haste or cowardice. Wimps don't find lost ponds. Perhaps, I considered, only idiots do. Taking five or six casual steps toward the stump of a dead tree, I eased off my backpack, opened it, and fished out my battered old copy of *My Sky*.

Cracking the book at random, and then sitting on the stump, I began to read aloud, and loudly.

"To live," I read in a clear but restrained voice, "is to prey. For all of life is predatory. Even vegetarians. A carrot itself is a hunter, stabbing its one orange talon deep into the meat of Earth, seeking to claim that which is not yet its own." I paused, then continued aloud. "The roots of a tree, like the open talons of a hawk, clutch the earth and feed. The human hand reached for food, for fuel, for fur clothing, prior to questioning right or wrong."

Closing the book, I stood up. And this time, I spoke without reading to inform the gunner, who was watching me and hearing me, of my name and purpose.

"My name is Kenneth Matson. I'm sixteen. And if I catch a rabbit from your snare, I will skin it, then cook it and eat it. But I would like to share the meat with you. Please?"

Waiting, statue still, I heard the words of my final threat echo away across the quiet pond water. Matson, I thought, you're really rolling the dice. What if, I asked myself, I'd been totally wrong from the start? Suppose this was *not* Lost Pond? Then the only thing lost could be my life.

Perspiring, I waited for a gun to explode.

"My Sky," I hollered out. Holding both my arms straight upward, into a pose of some primitive prayer, I yelled the two words once again. *"My Sky!"* I paused. "John S. Fay didn't write this book. *You* did!."

Someone laughed.

Twisting my head from side to side, my eyes combed the brush, everywhere I looked. No one. Yet I knew I'd heard a human mouth laugh. Hyenas didn't chortle in the Adirondacks. I cupped my hands to yell. "Please," I said loudly, "do not be afraid." This, I thought, is irony, spoken through a pair of sweaty palms.

Then I heard a strong voice reply. "I have rarely been

afraid of a lost and frightened boy."

The voice was husky, yet *female*. Along with its tatters of age, its gleaming rang out more brilliantly than a blend of sunlight and snow. To me, the colorful inflections were autumn's wind, defying winter. Even though I was no longer afraid, my entire body trembled. As the bones of my legs seemed to melt into blubber, my chin quivered.

"I'm not lost, or frightened. I've come, " I told the unseen woman, "to learn from you, Jo Silver." I sucked in a breath. "To beg you, please, to honor me with your company." I smiled. "And I didn't really mean what I said about stealing your rabbit."

"Perhaps you should, if you are hungrier than I."

Turning, trying to more or less face the hidden voice, I asked, "Isn't it crazy for us to argue over a rabbit which still runs free?"

The laughter came again. This time, I was a bit more sure of its topographical source. Off to my left. Slowly I walked that way. The pond was on my right. But, after more than twenty paces, I still saw absolutely no one. She still laughed at me. Now, her mirth seemed to steal up from behind me. It was laughter on a cat's paw. The cat was black in a midnight of mystery. I was fully confused.

"Where are you?" I yelled.

"Turn," she ordered me, "and walk away from the echo of my voice."

My heart sank. Had I hiked all this way to be now commanded to scram? To split?

"Come," spoke the old woman.

As the word meant the opposite of *go*, I came, picking up my pack enroute, walking slowly at the pond's edge toward nothing in particular. I walked for fifty yards, or so, and then for a hundred more. All I saw was pond shore to my left, woods on my right.

I stopped. "Where are you?"

"Keep on coming, boy," she said.

Ahead were several rocks, the largest being about the size of a one-car garage. As there was a path between two of the boulders, I followed it, skirted the rock shoulder, and saw a tidy entrance. It was constructed of small logs, gray, chinked with moss. A one-person dwelling that made no apology for its rustic simplicity. Its gray seemed a part of the rocks. The doorway was a small black hole, much like an entrance to a cave. I looked at the door, however, only for one brief glance as my eyes suddenly fixed on the woman who sat on its low roof.

"Welcome," she said.

Words wouldn't come to me. All I could do was stare at a smooth coppery face, two white braids of hair, a deerskin blouse, matching trousers, and mocs. A shotgun lay sideways across her lap, unthreatening, yet confidently ready. She appeared to be fit, able to outrun deer.

"Come closer," she told me.

I came. Where she sat was the hub, a vortex, of a natural granite megaphone. From here, her voice could speak in conversational tones, yet carry across all, or much, of Lost Pond. One glance, plus my brain, quickly solved that little mystery. I sighed, not knowing quite what to say as I dropped my pack to the ground to look fully at her. All I held now was my copy of *My Sky*. Then it hit me what I'd say to her. Because I knew her as a woman of wit as well as wisdom.

"Jo Silver Fox...I presume."

"Yes."

She smiled at me, shining her silvery eyes as they seemed to look at me inside and out. Jo Silver appeared older than I had expected from the outdated photography I'd seen of her college years at Mount Holyoke. Yet her voice sounded strong, confident, and her body looked trim. I couldn't guess her age, but I could see she was no longer young.

"You are quite a lad."

"Thanks," I said. "And thank you a million times more for allowing me to come and visit you." I held up my book. "After reading this, meeting you became part of my destiny. You, above all people, should easily understand that."

She nodded. "So I do."

I smiled at her, more with my heart than my face and lips. What happened next surprised me. With one smooth motion she jumped from the roof, landing lightly on her mocs, creating hardly any sound. Except two soft thuds.

"I knew you'd come," she told me.

"Me?"

She rested the butt of her shotgun to the earth, holding it casually by the end of its barrel. Then she held out her other hand to shake mine; stepping forward, I took it. Her fingers felt cool, tender, yet firm. I liked shaking her hand. Her silver eyes studied my face. But, for some reason known only to Jo Silver Fox, her hand rose to touch my cheeks and my hair. Gentle fingertips explored my face.

"So it's you, is it? Well, sooner or later, I knew *someone* would come. A reporter, perhaps. Or some lifelong friend whose nose was itching with curiosity."

"I sure am itching with curiosity," I told her.

"You came a long way. Boys of your age usually do not venture this far to meet a *young* woman, say naught of an ancient one." She touched my arm. "Tell me your name again."

"Kenneth Matson."

She repeated my name, slowly, as though trying to decipher its sound and meaning.

"Most people call me Kenny. By the way, what do I call you? What would you most *like* to be called?"

Her answer really jolted me.

"Mother," she said.

13

We stayed up late, talking.

Together we sat on moss, Jo Silver Fox and I, with our backs leaning against a pair of white birch trees, looking out over the darkness of Lost Pond. I worried that I was keeping her up beyond her usual bedtime.

"What time do you go to sleep?" I asked her.

"In winter."

For some reason, her prompt retort made sense to me. More so when she explained that during the warm months here, she was quite active. Earlier, the old woman had showed me the inside of her cave which, to my dismay, was a long tunneling den that led into the warmth of earth. This was how she had survived the merciless severity of so many icy and snowbound Adirondack winters.

"Why do you live here alone?"

"I choose to."

"In other words, you've come here to die."

"To live. Then to die."

"I suppose," I said, tossing a pebble into the black

water, aiming at the moon's midnight reflection, "you won't ever write another book."

Jo Silver shook her head, a gesture I could barely detect as we were sitting about seven feet apart. "I have sung my prayer," she said.

With my hands on each end of a short twig of birch, I bent it gently across my knees, thinking. "Well, I haven't," I said. "I can't promise that I'll grow up to be a writer, but I'm sure going to give it a go. It's one of the things I'm itching to be."

"What do you wish for most?"

I smiled in the dark. "Amy Woodward."

"Aha! A young lady, no doubt."

"Not that young. Actually she's older than I am."

"Is she? And how ancient is this creaking old crone of whom you so endearingly speak?"

"Seventeen. I'm sixteen. But that really doesn't bother me, or her, a whole lot."

"Indeed it shouldn't. What matters is that the two of you truly enjoy one another's company."

As she spoke, Jo Silver Fox looked over at me, her silvery eyes shining as though they were twin moons. But then, in the next instant, she caught me staring at her, and abruptly turned her head away, as though the old woman was trying to avoid my attention. It puzzled me.

"Tell me about yourself, Kenneth Matson."

I laughed. "There's very little to tell. I'm just a nobody kid. You're famous, and I'm a total unknown. Nobody knows me." Laughing again, I said, "I don't even know myself."

"Tell me anyhow."

"Okay. My mother teaches English and Dad sells real estate. I like to shoot pool, read books and sleep, but

I'm allergic to English walnuts. I live in Stamford, Connecticut, and go to school at North Academy in Lake Placid. I'm a lousy athlete and a worse musician. My grades are unsatisfactory, according to my teachers, because they tell me how bright I am, and that I ought to be a valedictorian instead of a weirdo."

"I already know how bright you are," she said, looking out across the quiet of the pond. "Because you *came*. You're the only one who did. And I'm glad."

"Thanks."

"And I'm very pleased that you've found your Amy Woodward. It's more important than finding me. Much more. Yes, I am *delighted* you found *her*."

"Me too."

"Like you, Kenny, I was once young and in love. We were chocolate and vanilla, my brown and his white. A penny and a dime. It hurts to recall our time together. So I don't let myself remember."

"Yet you do."

She nodded, stretching out a buckskin-clad leg as though trying to subside a cramp. "If you and your cherished Amy unite, never drive her away. Hold her to you forever. And tame the shrew in each other."

"Amy's not a shrew. She's as tame as I am."

The old woman looked at me and slowly shook her head. "I doubt seriously that a woman *you* would adore is tame at all. By the way, just how much do you know about shrews?"

"They're sort of like mice. Aren't they?"

I heard Jo Silver chuckle. "No, sweet lad, they are *not* at *all* like mice. Were a shrew to have only one synonym, it would be...*intensity*."

"Why?" I asked, chewing my birch twig's bitterness.

"A shrew knows neither night nor day. Her principal drive is hunger. Oh, every so often, she'll pause, close her eyes for half a minute, and sleep soundly. Rarely for much longer. Her metabolism is too intense to rest. She is a prowling appetite with red-tipped fangs. A shrew is today's *Tyrannosaurus,* only she is two inches long, and possibly weighs less than a nickle."

Listening, I didn't want to say anything to interrupt Jo Silver Fox. I wanted her to talk, talk, talk. My one anxiety was that I'd forget some of it. I was grateful to hear her continue.

"Her saliva is rife with venom. At rest, her heart beats, accept it or not, about thirteen hundred times a minute. But as she stalks and attacks her prey, which is often much larger and heavier than herself, a shrew's heart pumps at close to eighteen hundred times a minute. That, my son, is her intensity."

I smiled in the dark. "Golly, I wonder how many times Amy Woodward's heart beats when she looks at me."

The old woman was quick to reply. "Oh, I would imagine her heart reacts quite properly, on a *hunt.* The same as a shrew's."

"On a hunt? She's a *girl.*"

Jo Silver threw a scrap of white birch bark at me. I ducked. Yet I was still unprepared for such a sudden ferocity. "A male lion rarely hunts," she said stoutly.

"But they're all in Africa."

She looked at me evenly. "There are lions on this mountain, my boy. I hear them come, at midnight, to drink from my pond. Our pond. Their screech is unmistakable. Great tawny panthers called mountain lions, cougars, pumas, catamounts, or wildcats. They are lions."

"Are you ever afraid?" I asked the question because I wanted to hear her answer. I doubted she was afraid of anything. Nor had Jo Silver ever known fear.

"Yes," she said.

It startled me. *"You?"*

"Fear," she said, "is a facet of intelligence. Among us humans, perhaps fear is what we have in our brains in place of instinct. Or weaponry. An old woman who doesn't respect one of these powerful lions up here would be a simpleton."

"Will we see a lion tonight?"

"No, I think not. But I wager *they* have already seen *us*. And smelled us." My body flinched. "Don't fret. I smear bits of bear dung around the door of my lodge and other places. No, they won't come. Yet I imagine they now hear us as we chat. A lion can hear a bug snore."

I was trying my hardest to understand, and file away, all that Jo Silver Fox had been sharing with me. A lot of it made solid sense. But not all, so I asked her to explain about the bear manure.

"Aren't you afraid that bears will be attracted by their own scent and visit you?"

"Certainly not this time of year."

"Why not?"

"It's bedtime, or almost so, for our bear friends. Besides, in autumn, the bears are so fat from eating all spring, summer, and early fall, they're not hungry. Oh, they won't hibernate for several more weeks. Not until the snow comes. Bears adore playing in snow banks, like children. So you see, the lions dislike a bear smell, and the bears must dislike my scent."

"How did you learn all this stuff? At Mount Holyoke or from your father?"

Jo Silver was silent for a moment. "I have mostly learned," she said, "from God. From observing Her great family of living creatures and plants. There's only one truth. It is Nature. All else is tainted by human opinion, and therefore it is worthy of reassessment or discard. If you can learn only one thing, my young friend, *learn what is*. Education is often an outdoor adventure."

"I agree. So much of what they teach in school is about the world, or society, as some politician or scholar *wants* it to be. They always want to impose some new political system or social order. When I read or hear all that rot, it makes me want to barf."

As I spoke, I snapped the twig across my knees, breaking it in two.

"Perhaps that is why," she said, "I'm a hermit."

14

Hermit.

The word which Jo Silver Fox had spoken seemed to float across the blackness of Lost Pond, echoing, then returning to linger inside my head, pounding on my eardrums. A sound as lonely as its meaning.

It prompted an earlier question of mine which had been haunting me since I first arrived here.

"Why do you want to be called Mother?"

Jo Silver smiled. "Please pardon me for that, Kenny. I blurted honesty without thinking, and only remembering. Long ago, I gave birth, but my little girl died."

"I'm sorry. I figured that. Because it's near the end of *My Sky,* where you wrote about the evening sunset, and when a planet lost her moon. I sensed that it was a mother and a child. And the mother was you."

Her head bowed. "My body failed me. Afterward, I learned that I could conceive no more children. I'd hatched my only broken egg."

My thoughts about how Jo Silver felt when losing her child were interrupted by a screech, which came from a long way away.

"A panther," she said. "A mountain lion."

Its echo died, yet I could hear the lonely cry. It made me wonder why Jo Silver had written *My Sky* under the name of John S. Fay. So I asked her.

"That," she said, "was the beginning, perhaps, of my withdrawal from society. It's possible that using another name was a form of hiding from life. There's no other logical explanation, except that I was steeping in self pity. We all have weaknesses. But I could no longer face my own. So I wrote *My Sky,* partially hiding, and then fled. But there are other reasons why I became a hermit."

"Please tell me."

Her silvery eyes almost glowed in the moonlight. "I'll tell you. Years ago, when I was about your age, I was somewhat of a rebel. As a young student at Mount Holyoke College, I shocked the other girls by informing them that I wasn't a Christian. Instead, a Mohawk, and *my* religion was possibly older than theirs."

I nodded. "Well, that figures. What else?"

"However," she said, "I soon became fascinated by Christianity. Not because I admired the manners or behavior of my so-called Christian classmates, but because I was intrigued with the teachings of a young Hebrew carpenter of Nazareth."

"So you went to Yale Divinity School."

"Yes." Jo Silver rubbed her hands together as though preparing some unseen substance. "At Yale, I wrote a rather controversial treatise which won a prize."

"What about?"

She looked at me. "Corn."

"Corn?"

Jo Silver smiled. "Please remember, Kenny, that I'm half Mohawk. Centuries ago, before the white people came *to enlighten us,* Indians were already gardening, planting squash, beans, herbs, as well as corn. To a Mohawk's ear, and heart, the word *corn* is holy, as it is a gift of the Spirit. To me, more holy than a Bible, because corn is *entirely* of God's making."

As the echo of her words drifted away and into the night, I thought about what she was sharing with me. It made sense. I wanted to learn more about her philosophy of corn, and asked her to tell me.

"Like you," she said, "corn is golden sweet. It springs from rich earth, yet requiring a hoe and a harvester, and finally a thankful blessing at a supper table. Gratitude, my boy, is the highest note in the hymn of prayer. My father danced the Corn Dance, not to ask, but to give his thanks."

"Wow. I guess I know why your paper on corn won a prize. It's a ton."

The old woman laughed. "That *prize* kicked up a lot of dust among the Yale faculty. And in the years that followed."

"How come?"

Before answering, Jo Silver folded her hands, lacing her slender fingers together. "Oh, I guess because the second part, my sequel, stated that America was turning away from the sacred sweat of a cornfield, and too many Americans expected our government to work a hoe."

"I don't get it."

Jo Silver pointed at me. "All right, let's say that you are hungry. Your belly is starving for corn. Now our government can print food stamps, enact agri-law, create parity, influence corn prices, and even ban pesticide."

"How will all that feed me?"

"Exactly! It won't produce a kernel." Laughing, she clapped her hands. "For unless a farmer stoops, to sweat, plant, hoe, harvest, and truck his corn, he will *starve*."

Her voice hardened into bitterness. "So will an Indian when a government takes away his land. I'm afraid we Mohawks who know America's history put little trust in governmental promises. Believe me, the Indian knew about hunger."

Somewhere, from the darkness across Lost Pond, a hawk screeched. Perhaps it was an owl. A hungry belly was searching for meat. There was, I was thinking, something holy in the sound, a chapel bell of night. A hunting horn.

Jo Silver sighed. "Don't listen to me, Kenneth. I may pollute your young mind. If you do listen, please do not swallow it whole. Chew it, digest it with the juices of your own reason. For inside your brain, it will be *your* values which count, not mine."

"Okay."

"Now," said Jo Silver, "that you realize that a woman who runs away to live alone shouldn't intellectually be trusted, let's continue our conversation." She paused. "Do you know what attracted me so to the life of that Nazarene carpenter?"

"Tell me."

"Corn...from a sea."

"I don't understand the connection."

The old woman inhaled a deep breath, and then released it slowly, as though whetting my thirst for her thoughts.

"Jesus of Nazareth," she said, "enjoyed close friends. But the men He chose were not high-ranking officials, they were neither Sadducees nor Pharisees. Instead, they were Galilean fishermen. Men who sweated in their laborings, and no doubt reeked of fish and salt. In a way, His friends were peasants and reapers who had to gather corn from the waters."

Resting my chin on a bent knee, I said, "You know,

I'm not a very religious person. I skip chapel a lot. But I like what you're saying about the fishermen."

"Good." She laughed. "So do I. Tell me, Kenny, do you have a best pal at your school in Lake Placid?"

Her question made me think about my roommate, a big clumsy kid from North Carolina whose name was Jasper Boat. The guys called him Gunboat, because of his size. Sometimes, after lights-out, the two of us would talk. He'd always open up and share his secret feelings. I did too. Jasper was the only guy I told how I felt about Amy Woodward. And all he said was, "Gee, I wish I had a girl like that."

"Yes." I smiled to Jo Silver. "I got a pal."

"Well," she said, "our carpenter had a pal too. His name was Simon, a man I've always pictured as a thick, barrel-chested *brute*. A fisher. One who possibly sang bawdy songs and told the kind of jokes men tell. A common man."

"Is that what Simon was like?"

She shrugged. "Who knows. Certainly not I. Yet that's how I envision Simon, a giant rock of manhood."

I looked at her, and grinned. "You're sort of a rock of womanhood. To me you sure are. You aren't a silver trinket. You're iron ore."

Jo Silver Fox shook her head. "No," she said softly. "All I am is an aging halfbreed, one who is hardly certain of anything she tells you. So don't absorb anything I share with you on faith, because I have far more opinions than facts. You are young, and impressionable, so we can't let you leave Lost Pond to become a second *me*." She threw up her hands. "Heaven forbid."

"But," I said, "you *believe* in good things, like corn and sweat. A fisherman and a carpenter."

"You're a lamb."

It made me feel proud to hear her say it, even though

at North Academy, a lamb was a wimp, a sissy. But right now, I didn't mind the way she said it.

"Okay," I said, "I'll be a lamb if you want me to be one. But you're one heck of a lot more than an old halfbreed woman."

"Happiness, my lamb, is knowing what you are. Up here alone, I'm finally learning who I am. But what matters is who *you* are."

"Me?"

"I'm the past. In case you haven't heard, we Mohawks are obsolete. Dinosaurs of yesterday. But you are today and tomorrow. And if you cling to corn, fishermen, and carpenters, you'll find your way. And your craft."

"I'd like to become a writer."

"Wonderful. Tell me what you're writing."

"Well, I'm putting together some notes about a book on Nature."

"A vast subject."

"Sure," I agreed, "but *my* book will be about the natural way living things behave. Last year, I tried writing short stories and poems and stuff. But there's always so many *rules* to follow. That's the trial of being a kid. It's a tightrope of rules."

Jo Silver nodded. "Indeed," she said quietly, "I know. Because I broke every one. So I shall share with you a scrap of wisdom which my father, John Silver Fox, gave me. It's this. The only rules that really sculpt and shape you are the rules you enact for yourself."

"Nifty. I'm already doing that, which is sort of the reason I hiked up here to find you."

"Oh," she said, "you've made me feel so inadequate, because I've failed to give you anything of worth. Just my warped and twisted views on life. And whatever you do, Kenny, please don't gulp any of them down as gospel. Your mission, in this world, is not to emulate me in any fashion. Just be your own man. Your sky, Kenneth, not my sky."

Glancing at me, her silvery eyes seemed to be looking slightly over my shoulder, above my head, as if seeing the man I'd someday become. When I get back to North Academy, I thought, I'll tell Dr. Gray how I feel right now. How fortunate.

And about Jo Silver's corn.

15

We talked our night away.

Behind us, our fire was becoming ashes. The first hint of morning was starting to soften the black pond's surface into a cloudy pillow of gray mist. Yet I wasn't too sleepy. Only my back felt the hardness of the tree trunk upon which I leaned. Near me, Jo Silver Fox sat, dozing. Her eyes had closed and her handsome face appeared to relax. She looked to be perfectly at peace. Until both of us heard the *plop*.

Her eyes sprang open, instantly alert.

"There," she whispered, pointing at the pond's shore.

I looked, to see a small grayish animal at the water's edge, pawing among the wet leaves, stirring mud. The little beast growled.

"A possum," said Jo Silver. "One comes here every morning." She continued to whisper very softly. "It's one of the few animals I can't abide. Worse yet, I realize why."

"Why?"

"To be honest, it's envy."

I grinned at her. "You couldn't be jealous of a possum." Yet as I said it, I wanted to hear her reason.

"If that one's a female," she said, "she's spent her entire mature life pregnant. An absurdly short gestation period of less than two weeks, and then a prodigious litter. Sometimes even twelve or thirteen, each smaller than a bee. She'll bear more kits than she has nipples to nurse them."

Straining to see through the mist, I saw the possum had dragged a dead frog from the mud and was tearing into its white belly meat with her fangs. We continued to whisper.

"How do they all survive?"

Jo Silver Fox grunted. "They don't. She'll allow the weaker ones to starve and do little or nothing about it." She sighed. "I know. It's the way of Nature, of God. Otherwise, we'd all be wading up to our behinds in possums. But when I think of the hundreds of kits she'll bear, in her life span, and then remember how I couldn't produce even *one* living child..."

I recalled the passage in her book, one where a caterpillar curls up to hide, and becomes a dull gray moth. Colorless. Not a butterfly. "I guessed," I told her, "that somehow when I finally found you, that you might still be in some kind of motherly torment. In a way, I came to nurse you well again because of how I feel about my own mom."

"I know. You're a lamb of a boy."

It became difficult for me to talk, but I made myself do it. "I didn't come up here to announce my finding you to the world. It's too personal to brag about. In a sense, that would be as bad as making love to Amy and then mouthing-off about it to the guys."

She sighed. "Boys do that, don't they."

"Some boys do. *Men* don't."

Without speaking, Jo Silver fox moved closer to sit near me. I sort of expected her to hold my hand, or something; but she didn't. Her movement caused the possum to look up, then scamper off, away from the pond and into the brush.

"If you'll please pardon my saying so," I told Jo Silver, "you're worth saving."

Her silvery eyes widened. "Saving?"

"Maybe I didn't say it right. What I mean is, I don't know how I'm going to ever go back to Lake Placid and just *leave* you here. It's too wasteful. It would be like throwing away an apple after only one bite."

She smiled. "You're a delight."

"Well, I don't know about that, but at least I've always found myself, and my own thoughts, to be entertaining. I don 't *bore* me. You know."

Jo Silver pretended to give me a playful punch. "Yes, I do know. Because I have hardly ever bored myself. And we certainly don't bore each other. Do we?"

"No," I said. "We sure don't. You're my forever friend."

"Are you hungry?"

Suddenly I felt empty. "Very."

"Come," she said, getting to her feet with an agility that surprised me, even though she touched trees as she walked. "I have a rabbit hanging on a peg. We'll cook it for breakfast."

We walked to her lodge. Sure enough, a ripe rabbit hung there. As I touched it, the fur was soft, a bit damp from the night's dew; but its body was cold and wooden.

Jo Silver looked at me. "Build another fire, will you?"

"Right."

As the modest fire I'd revived was crackling and spewing its initial blast, unfit yet for cookery, the old woman tossed me the stiff animal. "Skin it," she ordered me. With a click I unsnapped the strap which held my hunting knife in its sheath. "And skin it with only your bare hands."

I knew how. Dad had once shown me, because, he'd said, it was necessary for me to master the arts of survival. Cracking the hind legs, I easily exposed two shafts of wet shining bone. Inserting my finger into each fracture-made vent, I parted the skin along each leg, up the belly, and tore the entire hide and head off cleanly. With a spreading yank of its legs, I ripped its underside and gutted it. Then I rinsed it in the pond and returned.

"There," I said. "Without a knife."

Jo Silver Fox nodded at me. "Good. Now roast it for us. Mind you, please don't ruin it. I don't intend to feast on black char on the outside and have the inside raw. Not with my old teeth."

I cooked it very slowly.

It took me so long that the aroma of the smoking meat cut into my yawning stomach, as if the dead rabbit was having some torturous revenge. The old woman squatted on her heels, watching and waiting, testing me with complaints on how hungry she was becoming. Yet she remained in one place for nearly an hour. Perhaps she was secretly lame, explaining why she reached for trees as she walked.

As the meat was roasting, I thought about some of the guys at school, the ones who mostly subsisted on burgers and fries. The fast-food freaks would turn up their noses at a rabbit, or snort their usual one-word comment, "gross," at the way I'd skinned and gutted it. I felt truly sorry for their limited view of life. They were Little Debbie eaters with Little Debbie brains.

I smiled. Amy Woodward packed more guts behind her belt buckle than a lot of the muscle guys at North Academy. No wonder I liked her so much.

"Ugly people eat ugly food," she'd observed, as the

two of us had been jogging by a Burger World.

Opening my pack, I broke apart my cooking kit, filled the pan with pond water, and boiled two helpings of my beans, because I wanted to give Jo Silver what was mine.

"I approve of you," she said finally, as though she were smelling the beans.

"At least of my cooking."

"Not only that. My father, as you know, wasn't a half-breed like me. John Silver Fox was all Mohawk. And he used to tell me, whenever he would roast a rabbit, that our patience was its gravy."

I pulled the rabbit off my fire. "It's ready," I told her. We sat on the ground. Still I did not use the knife, but gingerly tore off chunks of the steaming white meat, sharing it with her.

"Just put the plate beside me," she said. "I want the food to cool."

It was one of the best meals that I had ever eaten. Inside, I was trying to resist my pride in how I'd rid the rabbit of hide and guts, and cooked it to perfection. As I ate, I watched her use my fork (I used my spoon) and shovel beans into her mouth.

Watching her chew made me worry.

"You were hungry," I said. "You're going to grow old and feeble up here unless I stay and take care of you. Please don't frown at me that way. I just can't leave you here to starve."

She swallowed more beans. "What do you want me to do, Kenneth Matson? Return to the world, reside at some home for the elderly, and watch television?"

I sighed. "No, because by doing that, you'd sort of crush everything you've stood for or believe in. In a sense, you'd be polluting Lost Pond."

"Indeed," she said. "Living up here alone, Kenneth,

returns the balance to my life. I've had the outside world. And speaking of *balance*, it's the one thing I hope you discover and cherish."

As bean juice dribbled from my mouth, I used a sleeve of my shirt for a napkin. "Okay," I asked Jo Silver, "how do I balance Kenny Matson?"

She smiled at me. "Absorb from Nature as much as you do from textbooks."

"Is that what you meant by balance?" I asked, munching my boiled beans.

Jo Silver nodded. "Somewhat, yes. But balance the seesaw of your personal life with work and pleasure. In fact, find a path to an occupation which pleases you, and in your life, joy will abound."

"I'll try."

"Another thing," the old woman added. "Dirty your hands every day. It will cleanse your soul. Dig in soil to plant a flower, repair an engine, or skin a rabbit, and get to know *people* who earn their living by hard dirty work. During my own lifetime, I have gathered so much intellectual value from people who neither read nor write. In short, balance muscle with mind, and your hand will strum the harp of America's hymn."

I swallowed. Yet it wasn't beans which I was now trying to digest into my system. "Even though you're a hermit," I said, "you still love America, don't you? I feel you do."

"Truly, I do. Because the United States is all people. All values. We are God's proud garden of variety."

My face smiled impulsively. "Miss Fox, you're a closet patriot."

Laughing, she tapped the metal plate with the fork. "Quite so. I'm a sentimental cynic. Americans are the jewels of humankind. And if patriotism is corny, then I shall hug it all the more."

Looking at her, I said, "Instead of just sitting here, I ought to be writing all of this down on paper. Because my hiking up, meeting you, is the most awesome thing that's ever happened to me. Your book changed my life. In it, you wrote about the things I'd often thought about. It's like we're *related* somehow."

I bit into my last strip of hot rabbit meat.

"You sound to be quite a rebel," she said.

"Completely," I confessed. "At school, Dr. Gray calls me an academic terrorist. He and I are two of your biggest fans. It would really be great if you and Abe Gray could meet each other. In my opinion, he's the best teacher at North."

Jo Silver Fox nodded at me. "Good. I'm happy to be hearing how you respect your teachers."

I grinned. "In a way, everybody's sort of a teacher. You can soak up a lot of useful stuff from almost anyone you meet."

Setting down her dirty plate (*my* plate, actually), she moved to where I sat, touched me, and held my face between her hands. "I cannot explain this," she said, "because there's still so much of Heaven's magic we all have yet to learn. But do you know who you possibly are, in spirit?"

"No," I answered. "Who am I?"

Jo Silver smiled. "My daughter."

16

I grinned, but said nothing.

"You're not offended, are you?" she asked me.

"No, not at all. I'm not that fragile. Macho bores me as much as feminism. To prove it, I'll wash the dishes."

Gathering the pieces of my aluminum cooking kit, I grabbed my tiny bar of hotel soap from my pack, walked the few steps to the pond, and scrubbed everything clean. I whirled the clanking kit around in circles, to air-dry it over the fire before folding it away inside my pack.

"You must be exhausted," she said.

Suddenly I was. Yesterday, thanks to the pre-dawn arrival of Harley and Vernon, had been long in hours. Longer in uphill miles. Add to that, I'd stayed awake all night to chat with my idol. "I could use a nap," I confessed.

"Come," she said. "It's dark inside my cave. You can borrow my bunk and sleep all day, if you like."

That was when it happened! Earlier, I had noticed how Jo Silver had move about easily by her dooryard, as her hands touched the rocks. But this time, a new element, one that was strange to her, had been added. My backpack lay in plain sight between her and the door. Yet the old woman stumbled over it and fell. "Oh," she moaned. Then, as she lay on the bare ground with dirt on her buckskin suit, her voice began to regain its usual confidence. But somehow forced. "That was clumsy of me."

She sat up.

"You're not hurt, are you?"

"No," she almost snarled. "Of course not."

The morning had brightened, allowing me to look down into her face as I helped her to her feet. Her eyes were now beyond silver. They were more like icy ponds, or clouds. Knowing the reason she had tripped on my pack, which had been in full view, made me sweat. It explained her touching large rocks and trees as she walked.

"You're blind," I said softly.

She stared at me, seeing, I now guessed, merely my outline. Or nothing. The milky curds in her eyes were possibly cataracts. Now it made sense. As my mind perceived it, in seconds, I now realized everything that she had done she'd performed by feel or by hearing. Jo Silver Fox had lost her sight.

"I'm sorry," I told her.

She sighed. "Please don't *pity* me, Kenneth. I can't stand an overload of sympathy from people I like." Her hands were busily brushing the grit from her buckskins. "Besides," she added, "it should be obvious to you that I live alone here, so I'm certainly not *helpless*."

I rested a light hand on her shoulder. "Nobody said you were helpless. Only blind."

She looked at me. "I didn't want you to know," she said. "I was afraid to have you hand me a plate of food."

Bending, I picked up my orange backpack, wanting to kick it, or boot myself, because I'd accidentally embarrassed her. "But I *do* know," I said, "which is one more reason, now that I've found you, I can't leave you here."

Her face tightened. "Why not?"

My lungs inhaled so I could let out a long and troubled sigh. Never, my parents had advised, try to make an important decision when you're dog tired. Do it rested. So, instead of thinking, I yawned. I made sure to do it with sound effects, so Jo Silver would hear my yawn. Possibly she'd know I was now bargaining for time. Or for rest.

"Go to sleep, Kenneth Matson."

"I will. We'll debate it all later, okay?"

Jo Silver shook her head. "No, let's not."

Hanging my pack on the peg where the rabbit had been, I ducked through the tiny doorway, entered her cave, and flopped down on the one short bunk that seemed to be almost burrowed back into its own earth tunnel. It felt warmer there. Then I sat up to loosen my boots, pulling them off; smelling the stink of my socks was the final act I could remember. Yet I felt her cover me with a rough blanket, then leave.

"Blind," I whispered, as I drifted off.

I slept.

When I awoke, the stiffness in my body told me that I'd slept the entire day. Sitting on the bunk, I blinked, looking for Jo Silver Fox. "Hello?" I asked the darkness. Hearing no answer, I got to my feet, picked up my boots then padded in my stocking feet to the small open doorway, feeling my way as the place was unlit. I stumbled outside and spoke. "Miss Fox?"

I then heard her answer. "Outside," she called.

Having been asleep, my eyes were accustomed to darkness, so I located my hostess near the pond. She sat with her legs bent, knees outward, holding objects in her lap. As her head turned my way in a welcome, her white hair appeared light blue in the soft moonlight. Squinting as I approached her, I asked Jo Silver what she was doing.

"Making a banjo," she answered.

"Honest?" I knelt for a closer look.

"Yes. This isn't my first one. I've made others. Oh, it'll be a very crude instrument. But it will create music good enough for me."

Reaching out my hand, I slid my fingers along the smooth tapering neck. "How come there aren't any frets?"

"It won't need any. Because, you see, I know only a few basic chords. Nothing too fancy, or classical. Just mountain music."

"Wow."

Jo Silver raised her banjo a few inches. "All it takes is a hickory ring, a hide, and a holding hoop to form the drum. As to the neck, I tried sinking frets into a neck, long ago, but I never quite spaced them correctly, which resulted in discordant chords."

Ping! She tapped the drum with a fingertip.

"What kind of animal hide?"

"A cat." She grinned up at me. "Even though I'm blind, I can almost read the surprise on your face, Kenneth."

"You mean a house cat?"

Jo Silver nodded. "No, I didn't kill it. The cat, for some odd reason, wandered up here to my lodge, stayed for a few days, and died. I fed it, but the creature wouldn't eat. Too old. So I skinned it, and soaked and stretched the hide the way I had done with a squirrel."

"Then did you stretch the cat hide on the drum hoops, to dry into shape?"

"Exactly, after soaking it in ash water, for curing."

"What about the strings?"

"Deer gut, from a long-ago forkhorn I shot for food. Intestine, pulled tight and thin by weighting with rocks. Simple. And once the pegs fit the holes at the upper neck, all you have to do is twist and pound firmly. But the pin shaft ought to be long enough to reverse the tap to loosen it, for retuning. Unlike a ukelele, a banjo is tuned in fifths...G - D - A - E. Quite simple."

Touching a peg, I said, "But you're not using any tools. Are you?"

"All that's required is a knife. Nothing more."

As I watched, Jo Silver Fox attached a long length of deer gut to the drum's rim, ran it along the neck and around a peg which she turned to tighten it. It was almost impossible for me to believe that a blind person could handmake a crude banjo so skillfully.

"I suppose you work on it every day," I said.

"Daytime," she said, "is my night now. At night is when I perform all my necessary chores, and hobbies. It is Nature's way, you know. So now this elderly mole has become a nocturnal animal."

I nodded. It was true, I thought; for purposes of her own safety, she moved around mostly at night. Being blind wasn't so brutal a blow for her to accept in darkness. A thought struck me. "How," I asked her, "do you know if it's night or day? Can you tell the difference?"

She smiled. Her head easily fell back to rest on the trunk of a small white birch. "Oh, that's no problem at all. My pond is a clock of sound. Listen!"

I heard the bullfrogs and their deep jug-o-rum croaking.

"It's evening," she told me. "Later, when the deer tiptoe down to drink, I sometimes can hear an antler rub against a tree. But only if the big buck comes with

I didn't sing any more songs. Instead, eyes closed, I listened to Jo Silver's banjo, and knew that at this moment I was the luckiest kid on earth.

All I was missing was Amy.

17

The deer came.

Off to my right, I saw a herd of tan shadows, moving quietly to the shore of the pond. I whispered to Jo Silver. "The deer are coming to drink."

"How many?"

It wasn't easy to count them underneath only moonlight. I saw three mature does, two fawns. That was all. I reported my tally to the blind woman who sat at my side holding a handmade banjo.

I asked, "Where's the buck?"

"Be patient. You'll see him. He will be the last one to come. A buck will let his females drink first. But he's there, standing back in the shadows."

"Will they hear us talking?"

Jo Silver shook her head. "No, because the wind is blowing our way, from them to us. They won't smell us either."

What she said caused me to realize that I was beginning to smell myself, as I hadn't had a shower since Tuesday evening. Tomorrow would be Saturday. My salty shirt was about ready to be either boiled or buried, along with its ripe occupant. Soon I'd be smelling like a car which had run over a skunk. Thinking about my own cleanliness, or lack of it, made me wonder how Jo Silver Fox kept herself so clean. No doubt she had her own bathing habits, personal ones, into which I decided not to pry.

"Can you see the buck yet?"

"No," I said, "there's no sign of him."

But just as I said it, the big boy made his appearance. He was too far away in the dark for me to count the points on his rack. Yet I could see those antlers, quite clearly; he held his head aloft, knowing that he was a king beneath his thorny crown.

"There he is," I whispered.

"He's not drinking yet," said Jo Silver, her eyes closed as she whispered. "He will stand very still while his nose and ears determine danger or safety. His head will turn, slowly, to sweep the shores to the left and to the right."

"That's right! It's *exactly* what he's doing."

I was amazed how this blind and beautiful lady could *see* so much, without sight. The vision of her memory and her vast knowledge was still so clearly in focus.

"Right now," Jo Silver Fox continued to whisper, "the does and fawns are all watching him. None of them are drinking. Nor are they browsing on the unhatched autumn buds that tip the cascading birches. See, my boy. *See* how they respect their monarch."

Squinting, I couldn't see the faces of the does or their fawns, yet I somehow felt and knew all that Jo Silver was telling me.

"There can be no sweeter beauty," she said, "to compare to how the soft brown eyes of a doe admire her lord. Unless, of course, it is the way he also looks at her."

Reaching over, I touched her hand. I didn't have to say anything. She already knew.

"Kenneth," she whispered, "bring your Amy Woodward to watch deer. Do it soon. And, as the deer silently come to drink their cooling pond water, hold your young Amy close to you."

"I will."

"Gather her beneath the curve of your arm and shoulder. Then lower your head, ever so gently, and touch your nose to hers. It is a Mohawk's gesture. There will be no need for you to explain your caress. She will answer."

Watching the buck's antlers slowly fall as he bowed to his thirst, I said, "Thank you, Jo Silver Fox."

Her hard fingers squeezed my hand. I felt her strength again, a proud feeling. Inside, I wanted Amy Woodward to be here too, plus Dr. Gray and my parents, so all could be nourished by the company of so magnificent a lady.

"I'm glad you came," the old woman said as she leaned closer to my ear. "You see, I'd forgotten how to share my deer, or my rabbit, with another worthy person."

She shivered once in the October air.

"Are you cold?"

"Hardly at all," she answered. "And only on the outside. Inside me, my heart is warm. In a fashion, I'm storing up heat."

I thought of the rattler. "Like a snake on a sunny rock?" I asked her.

"Yes, as the deer now drink, perhaps these are my last precious sips of living, cool and clear. But I have lived fully, and loved. I feel a taste more tangy, now that I can hope my seeds will survive in you, Kenneth Matson."

It was my turn to squeeze her hand. Yet, as I did so, it wasn't quite enough. So I leaned close to her, touching the tip of her nose with mine.

"Bless your heart," she said.

"And yours."

"Kenneth, there is a task, an unpleasant one, that I am going to ask you to perform for me. Only one."

"A task?"

"Yes. I will die in my cave."

"No, you can't..."

With a sudden fervor, she stiffened her body as if to defy my objection. "Listen to me! Please." Her outburst spooked the deer. In less than a second, the tawny shadows became blurs of departure. The herd of chimes was ringing on the rocks and then stilled.

"I'll listen."

"Good. Above my lodge...look around and you'll see it...is a granite boulder. Too heavy to lift. Yet, if you fell a small tree, and sharpen one end, you'll be able to dislodge it."

"Why?"

"Be patient. When it falls, close to my dooryard, again use your pole to roll it to my door. It will fit. I have measured it many times. As the ground slants toward the door, this granite should forever seal my lodge."

"I understand."

"Then you will return someday to close my tomb forever?"

"Yes, on my honor."

Jo Silver patted my shoulder. "Good."

I didn't like hearing what the old woman was requesting that I do. Not a bit. The feeling made me partially regret that I'd so quickly agreed to do it. Then, somehow in her darkness, she must have sensed my reluctance.

"It won't be easy for you, Kenneth...the climb, finding me dead, moving that rock and then leaving."

"No," I said. "It certainly won't."

"Yet you are man enough." As she spoke, her resolute fingers bit into the muscle of my upper arm. "Man enough."

Nodding, I thought about Dr. Gray, back at North. He'd warned me, just before I'd caught the bus on Wednesday, that perhaps I wouldn't be ready for learning all that I would possibly learn. He'd been accurate. There was, I still knew, more to her story. But I had decided not to pester an old woman. Inside, she was a rock. There was, however, a crack in this mass of granite soul, from which a shrub of a child, her daughter, had long ago sprouted.

I sighed, looking at her.

"No," I told her, "I can't be your daughter, because I have to be who I am. I'm Kenny Matson of Stamford. There's no Mohawk blood in me. Not a drop, as far as I know."

Jo Silver touched my arm. "As to your being my daughter, you're certainly bright enough to realize that I didn't mean that in the physical sense."

"I know that."

"But that's an adequate explanation for you. Or is it? I feel your hunger to know more."

I stared at her. "You *do*?"

She nodded her coppery face. "Oh, I sense that rather deeply. So I will share my destiny with you, kind sir, if you'll listen."

"I'm all ears."

I was holding my breath, imagining that I was solving the one riddle in *My Sky* that had so haunted me. The twin clouds and a rainbow.

"Yesterday," she said, "I called you my spiritual

daughter. Even though you're a young man."

"Why?" I asked her.

Her blind eyes looked up at the stars, perhaps seeing more than I, or anyone else, could ever see. "I called you *daughter,* because...no sooner had you arrived...I knew you were my lanyard."

"Lanyard?"

"Yes, because you are my stout leather thong, linking me to a past from which I ran. But more, connecting me to a third person. Someone whose face is only a blur. A face with no name."

As I scratched the back of my neck, the itch of my intellectual confusion seemed to be biting. Like a gnat. Perhaps, I thought, if I read *My Sky* again, the jagged pieces of this lady's life would be guided into order. There had been, I recalled, a passage about a lace of leather, a lanyard from a deerhide robe. So absorbed was I among the ill-fitting parts of this jigsaw, that I had not been aware that I now sat alone by Lost Pond.

I looked around. Jo Silver was gone.

"Where are you?"

Then I saw her, returning in the dark from her cave, walking slowly, and touching the trees to guide her. In her hand she was carrying something. As she came to me, I saw what it was.

"This," she said, "was to be my bridal dress. It's white buckskin, from an albino deer."

It looked yellow now, as I took a closer look. But I would never tell her so.

"It's very white," I said. "And pure."

Sitting beside me, with the dress in her lap, her fingers found a seam. As it was frayed, she pulled a leather thread from it, then snapped it off, handing it to me.

I took it.

"Since my childhood, Kenneth, I've always been able

to predict many of the events in my unusual life. I know it may sound spooky to you, but the tiny length of leather I just gave you isn't for *you* to keep. You may have an opportunity to...to share it with someone."

"Who?"

"I don't know. That shall be your decision. All I can tell you is that you and I are not alone up here."

"But I don't understand."

"You soon may."

18

I slept again.

This time, not in Jo Silver's lodge. I fell asleep at the edge of Lost Pond with my head in her lap. Beneath my face was a soft pillow of faded buckskin.

"It's time," she told me.

Even before opening my eyes, I knew the nudge of morning. I heard birds. Also, my nose smelled the sharp sting of wood smoke. In the night, the old woman had built a fire nearby so the two of us wouldn't freeze during the chill of October. I sat up, my body fighting the cramps in my back. My legs felt wooden.

"It is time, Kenneth Matson, for you to leave. Return in late April, or May. The bears and I shall possibly be awake by then."

I tried to smile. "Promise?"

Jo Silver smiled. "I shall survive, my boy, as long as God wills a use of me down here. The decision is neither mine nor yours. It is Her choice, for She is the Mother of all. So it's best we children harken to Her silent statutes, and obey."

We ate together. She treated me to a hot stew which she had prepared in a black kettle, over her fire. The pottage contained, according to the information from my scalding tongue, a blend of fish and wild onions, an antithesis of Burger World. I ate gratefully, silently, considering it improper to ask what it was. Its brutal flavor tasted strange, untamed, bordering on savage, seasoned by a leaf or two of spice, plus some uncivilized hunks of root.

"You'd better get started, Kenneth."

Reluctantly, I loaded myself into my orange backpack. The tightness in my throat prevented my saying any words. Jo Silver would understand, as she had understood all living creatures, save one. Herself. I held up the leather thread she had given me. Then, feeling like a fool because she had no sight to see it through her milky eyes, I said, "Don't worry, I'll carry your thread buttoned inside my pocket."

"Thank you, my sweet lamb."

I'm not a lamb, I wanted to tell her; nor am I your daughter. And I hope I can be your lanyard. But I don't even deserve even one of these distinctions. As I could fritter away no more early daylight, there was no time to argue.

"Johanah Silver Fox," I said, looking at how strongly beautiful she really was, "I'll miss you."

She smiled. "And I shall treasure this visit. Oddly enough, I have always wanted special friends to call me Johanah. Yet only a chosen few."

Saying nothing more, I walked to her, opened my arms and hugged her about as hard as I could. I'll be back, my arms were telling her, knowing she would understand. Her fingers blessed my face.

"Good luck to you, Kenneth Matson. And thank you for being that one unique person I hoped you would be. My lanyard, and my lamb."

I waved to her, feeling that she would somehow sense that I was doing it, in her blindness. I had to hold my guts together when I saw her wave back, reaching her hand high into some mysterious dungeon of night that only a blind person knew.

Sun lightened her white hair.

Hiking like a dead machine, feeling nothing, not even the weight of my pack, I passed the flat rock where I had seen the rattlesnake, knowing I was on my way home. Or rather, back to school. My boots each seemed to be anchors. My brain heavier with guilt and worry. Compared to the weights of the mind, I was thinking, a backpack is a dandelion seed, wafted by wind. Yet, I knew, going back to North was my only choice. Because I wasn't going to insult Jo Silver, telling the old woman that she was too unfit, too incompetent to hack it alone. Besides, she was the most stalwart human individual ever to breathe air, male or female. Jo Silver Fox was granite. And tears.

A loon piped.

It was all I could do not to glance back over my shoulder, to the west, in the direction of Lost Pond. Looking up, I wondered if I would spot the eagle again. Or the osprey. Better they, I was deciding, than a return encounter with those two charming citizens of Pine Corners, bully old Harley and whining Vernon.

I laughed.

How I'd enjoy inviting Vernon to visit me, in Stamford, and then introducing him to Mom as my North Academy roommate. "That's it, Matson," I said. "Don't fracture your funnybones. Just keep laughing up here, all by yourself." According to stereotype and legend, that was what lunatics did in the woods. They ran through mountain forests, grinning and giggling, lost in their own mad maze of idiocy.

By noon, judging from the sun's highest autumn position, I had crossed the flat granite. Mid-afternoon found me approaching the high lip of the ledge. I had used the twin castles, which I now called His and Hers, as my landmarks, so that I would hit the crest of the uppermost ledge near where I'd scaled it.

The osprey cried from somewhere distant. "Bug off!"

Well, I thought, that doesn't mean Matson's on target. Consulting my compass, I learned next to nothing of use; its needle appearing to be on vacation, or spaced-out on iron ore. Lode, Mr. Clepp had called it. So my compass was loaded on lode.

It made me laugh out loud, only one time, because the twin castles laughed back. Hearing the echo gave me chills.

Foolishly, I had forgotten to mark the place where I had earlier conquered the steep climb up the ledges. Nothing looked familiar. One cannot use the blade of a hunting knife to notch granite. Shedding my pack, I sat, chewed juniper berries and tried to plan a downward trip. And *trip* was hardly an encouraging word. One false step down there and I'd get myself mashed, like a dropped bomb.

"Panic time?" I asked aloud.

No, not this kid. I smiled. Because old Kenny Matson had actually pulled it off, found Lost Pond, and met a majestic lady. I suddenly realized that Johanah Silver Fox was the only famous person I'd ever met, one on one. Politicians didn't count. Dad had once remarked, "Politicians are nothing special. They're mostly lawyers who couldn't hack it in private practice."

My parents were really okay people.

Maybe they weren't famous. But nobody could accuse Shirley and Sam Matson of white flagging. They both really put out. Up at six every morning. Thinking about Mom and Dad made me realize how much I missed them, and how foolish I'd been, meandering up here into nowhere. Anything could have pulled the pin on me: the osprey, a rattlesnake, adding to that the fact that Jo Silver could have been crazy, not blind, and shotgunned my rear-end off. Then, in addition, there was Harley and Vernon.

Or, I grinned as I thought, the irresistible Miss Bessie Quill, beyond whose scarlet door I would have fallen to charms that could have kept me there, perhaps willingly, forever.

I ate my final hunk of flat bread. Some of it had turned a bit green with mold, but that part was merely flicked off by my thumbnail. Lost Pond, and its environs, was no place for a lost kid to waste chow. The bread tasted rather stale, slightly better than gnawing wall plaster, but not much. Its rough edges hurt my mouth, and I had to let my saliva slowly soften it, prior to swallowing.

Would I be able to find the spring again? The drying thought of thirst had begun to nag me. No hurdle. I was only two days, actually a day and a half, from the endearing comforts of Pine Corners hospitality.

I felt for my wallet! It was still in my back pocket. At least I could patronize Libby Potter's grocery to partake, once again, of her magnetic personality. If her brother and Vernon would allow.

Getting up, I worked a kink out of my right leg, pulled on my pack, and pointed my nose toward the ledge.

Selecting a tiny fragment of granite, I threw it, hard and far as I could, out into nothing but Adirondack air, to watch it fall, down, down, spending itself from an arc into a plummet. The rock made no sound as it eventually crashed, out of view.

"Let's go, sport," I said. "You don't have time to waste on baseball practice."

Working my way down, ledge after ledge, I recalled reading about mountain climbers. It was harder, they'd claimed, to go down instead of up. As my boot toe probed for each elusive foothold, I had to agree. Fear of falling made my body sweat. Several times, I doubted that I'd make it, because so much water trickled from the cracks, causing my fingers to slip.

The pack had started to torture my shoulders. Every muscle ached and my legs had become limp noodles. The danger was increased by the fact, as I faced the rocks, that my backpack constantly pulled me backwards.

"One slip," I told myself, "and I could smash."

Perhaps, I thought, the fall wouldn't kill me, and I'd lie there for days, hollering for help, and gradually dying. The vision of a broken spine or leg soaked my body with perspiration.

I got totally stuck on one ledge, unable to proceed, neither up nor down. Removing my pack with extreme care, I used one hand to hold a ragged-edged crack; with the other, I threw my pack, watching it fall silently and disappear.

Lighter now, I skidded my belly downward, clawing at every granite protrusion which could halt my fall. My hands felt raw and burned. It was almost dark when my body scraped down the last fifteen feet or so, ripping both trousers and shirt.

My backpack lay there beside me, as though staring at me in disbelief that I'd landed.

I had no water to boil coffee. The last of the ham I figured, would heighten my thirst, so I resisted eating it. Besides, remembering Jo Silver, I felt too empty to eat. So I prepared camp.

Unrolling my sleeping bag, I untied my boots, pulled

them off, winced at the stink of my socks, then crawled into my bag.

I prayed, thanking God for watching over Jo Silver Fox and me, and then adding Mom, Dad, and Amy Woodward. Lying alone, in the silence of night, I couldn't force myself to close my eyes. I heard an owl's hoot. If the owl was small, I was in no danger. A great horned owl, Dad claimed, would attack a moving-van, if the owl was hungry. It would even battle an eagle and win. I was longing to hear some sort of go-to-sleep music. A kid's whim. So I imagined my listening to Amy playing her flute. For a brief moment, I was home in our living room in Stamford, Connecticut, reading some of my mother's poems.

It didn't work. I can't sleep when I'm hungry, thirsty, tired, scared, or nuts. I must have rolled, in search of a comfortable position, for at least half of the night, then, out of sheer exhaustion, finally drifted off.

There was early daylight when I opened my eyes and saw a man.

He stood close to me, about ten yards away. At first, I saw his boots, trousers, a woolen buffalo-plaid shirt that was a black and red checkerboard. Then his face. I couldn't belive who he was. Sitting up, I rubbed my eyes, stared at him again, and spoke his name.

"Dr. Gray?"

19

He yanked off his cumbersome pack.

"Kenny! Thank the good Heaven I found you," he said. "I've been searching for you since Friday noon, yelling your name, and hearing nothing but an echo."

Dr. Abraham Gray leaned heavily against a tree trunk, appearing too exhausted to squat. He needed a shave. In addition, his posture appeared as though he'd been run over by a slow truck.

"Are you all right?" he panted.

"Of course. What day is it, sir?"

"Sunday." My old prof sat awkwardly on a fallen log, fumbling into a pocket of his woolen parka, pulling out his pipe. Then he returned it to his pocket, without smoking. "I somehow sensed you were lost. Perhaps we both are." He looked slightly confused and tired.

I grinned. "Sir, I am not lost."

"You're not, eh?"

Still inside my sleeping bag, I raised myself up to lean on one elbow. "No, sir. I'm on my way back to Pine Corners. Tonight, I planned to telephone my parents, and then phone you." My brain was beginning to awaken, and I couldn't wait to tell old Honest Abe my news. So I took a deep breath, smiled with satisfaction, and then told him. "Mission accomplished, sir."

As I saluted, his jaw dropped slowly open and I waited for the question, in words, which his deeply-lined face was already asking. "Did you actually *find* her?"

I nodded.

He stood quickly. "Where?"

"Lost Pond. I found *that* too."

Dr. Gray chewed his lower lip. Shoulders hunched, his entire body curved into a human question mark. "You *found* her?"

"Honest."

"Matson, if this is one more of your devilish pranks..." He paused for breath. "Please," he said, "don't fake it."

"I'm not, sir. I found Jo Silver Fox." With a grunt, I dragged my stiff body out of my sleeping bag, and tried to stand as tall as my towering announcement. "And sir, I didn't get lost."

Dr. Gray looked me up and down. "Your clothes," he finally said, "look as if you've been clawed by a bear. Are you positive you're all right?"

"I'm fine, sir."

"And...she is alive?" After I nodded, Dr. Gray looked up at the early morning sky. "Johanah is alive," he said in a whisper.

The way he said it suddenly answered one of the questions that I'd asked myself about him. His feeling for Jo Silver ran deeper than mere literary or scholarly respect. It was emotional. I was still sort of half asleep, and wanted to crawl back inside my sleeping bag for another week. The quicksilver suspicion, however, that Dr. Gray cared deeply for Jo Silver, was prodding me. My thoughts couldn't solidify into a casting of words.

As I studied Dr. Gray's face, *his* feelings for her seemed to be replacing my own.

"I mentioned you to her, sir."

Dr. Gray shrugged. "My name means nothing to her. She's a famous lady, or was. I'm just a prep school prof. That's all. Only a face in the crowd of admirers. Over the years, I've seen her only at a distance. I have never even shaken her hand."

I took a deep breath. "Dr. Gray, I'm only guessing, but I think you and she are...a lot closer than you realize."

He frowned. "I don't understand."

"Sir, neither do I. It's all rather cryptic. Maybe that's why it could be so exciting for the two of you. I'm not trying to be mystical. I'm too tired. So I'm guessing that some friendships are inevitable."

Mouth open, my teacher stared at me. "Strange," he said at last, "how you understand so much, for someone so young." He looked away. "I resented you, you know, envious of your courage to find her, your boldness in attempting my dream. She's the reason I never married. For years, I've been caring for her, secretly, ever since college, where I first saw her, at a dance. She was waltzing. But I was too timid to cut in."

I smiled. "I know, sir. Because I've finally sorted it all out. It's nuts, in a wonderful and romantic sort of way. And there's another bit of news that's even crazier."

He looked at me. "And what's that?"

"Sir...I'm your daughter," I said. "Please don't be alarmed. She told me I was, in spirit. I'm hers, and I'm yours. You and Jo Silver are kind of my godparents. It's all insane, and I'm too exhausted to explain it correctly, or even kindly. Maybe it's because I respect both of you so much."

Without speaking, Dr. Gray stumbled a step or two

toward me, holding out his right hand. His eyes were shining.

"Thank you, Kenny." His left hand ruffled my hair. "You," he said, "are one little Titan of a lad."

"You're welcome," I told him, too tired and confused to say more. But then I remembered something, and flipped open the button on the shirt pocket, pulling out the leather thong. "Jo Silver gave me this, to pass along to someone she has never met, yet likes. It's for you, Dr. Gray. I just know it is."

He took it.

"You never got married, sir?"

"No. I was always too shy. Too reluctant to pursue the only woman I ever really wanted."

"This thread," I told him, "is from a buckskin, albino-deer bridal gown. Jo Silver didn't marry either. She called me her lanyard, so I guess I'm a thread which ties her to you."

Dr. Gray swallowed. "How can a man my age still be in love with a lady he's never really met, or touched?"

"That day in your office, sir, when you told me that someone else ought to search for her, I knew it was you. It's fate, sir. Not something we learn in books. So never allow formal education to stunt your growth."

As he sat slowly on a rock, almost dazed, his fingertips began to caress the short length of white leather. Then he stopped. I went to sit close to him, so he'd know that I'd always be his friend, and that I was somebody he could trust with a secret. The deepest secret of his life.

"It's all in *My Sky*," I told him, "as you already know. You just didn't realize, sir, that I was the lanyard, the cord to connect the two souls. Remember the rainbow which follows the storm, and it spans the two lonely clouds? Well, I'm it."

Head bowed, Dr. Gray covered his face with his hands. "I recall," he said quietly. "Johanah wrote that passage long after her daughter...Bless you, Kenny, for finding her. And helping me to find myself. To be honest."

My fist pounded his bony old shoulder with an easy punch. "All along, I thought I'd be finding her for *me*. But I guess, sir, it was really for you."

"Is she all right?"

"Jo Silver Fox," I said, "is one of the most all-right people on Earth." I inhaled deeply. "Except for..."

"Except for what?"

"She's blind."

He gasped. "No!"

I nodded. "She's living all alone in a cave at Lost Pond, blind, and yet more capable of surviving than any animal or person I've ever had the honor of meeting. But, if you'll pardon my advice, sir, I think you ought to hike up there and visit her."

"Yes," he said. "I shall go...someday. But first, I'm escorting you back to Pine Corners and shoving you on a bus to Lake Placid."

Grinning, I shook my head at him. "No, sir, not someday. Today! Because I'm not lost and I know my way back." To prove it, I pointed east.

Dr. Gray looked where I pointed. "Are you sure?"

"I'm dead sure. Pardon my saying so, sir, but I'm a lot less lost than you are. And I wonder if I can let you climb up to Lost Pond by yourself. I could be your guide."

Suddenly, as I talked, I felt as though I was the teacher and he was my pupil. Studying his awkward pack, it became obvious that Dr. Gray was no woodsman. Perhaps he belonged in a classroom at North Academy, not in a wilderness. But his next remark changed my mind.

"Kenny, are you positive you know your way back to Pine Corners?"

Nodding, I said, "Sir, better than you know the way to Lost Pond. It won't be easy. You'll never lug that oversized pack of yours up there."

"Yes," he said calmly, "I will." His sudden resolute voice convinced me. "I know," he then added, "to you, I'm a gray old Dr. Gray, too much of a ninny to do what you did. You rascals at North ought to be calling me Dishonest Abe."

There was no stopping him, I thought, and it was all my fault for telling him to go. Yet were he not to try it, his respect for himself would forever haunt him. Perhaps destroy him.

"Maybe, sir, we both ought to get started. You up, and me down. Do you have a compass?"

He nodded.

"Don't trust it, sir. Use the sun, because there's iron ore up there." I pointed upward. "Climb these rock ledges between the twin peaks. Up on top, go west. When it gets dark, sleep,. You'll have to rest, sir, really. Then continue west, following a chain of clearings, downhill. And keep hollering one name...Johanah. Only special friends call her that."

"I'll do it."

"If she hears you, she might fire off a shotgun to guide your progress, but that's only a guess. Sir, you're about to meet a beautiful lady."

"All I have of her is a few press clippings. But I presume she's still lovely as ever."

I smiled. "You won't believe how much."

Together, we repacked his pack. I discarded some of his heaviest gear, and supplied him with some of mine, and all of my food, added to the generous amount he already had. I wouldn't worry about chow, because I knew Jo Silver Fox could make do for two. I warned him to stop, eat, rest, to pace himself, or he might never make it. Yet I knew he would. Dr. Gray was now more than a woodsman. He was totally Honest Abe.

It would be, I thought, Dr. Abraham Gray's final exam, a test of himself.

His face, as I watched him shoulder his pack, appeared very determined. Then, as he turned to flash a smile at me, I could hardly ask my next question. My throat was too tight.

"You won't be returning to North, will you, sir?"

Dr. Gray shook his head. "No. But give me two weeks. Then donate my clothes to the Good Will and my books to the school library. Except for *My Sky.* I want you to keep that one. Yours is torn. Upon your return, Kenny, go directly to Dean Stockton. He and I are friends and have been for years, so you can level with him. Straight out. I want the school to have my pension. And that's all I own in this entire world, except for my golden memories of some wonderful boys."

"I'll do it, sir. Count on me."

Resting a thin hand on my shoulder, he spoke in a raspy voice. "You were my favorite kid, Kenny. A rascal, yet I somehow picked you as the king of the crop."

"You're the best too, sir." I could hardly say it. "You're the finest teacher at North. In fact, you're right up there next to Mom, Dad, and Jo Silver."

As he held out his right hand again, I suddenly knew that a farewell handshake just wouldn't be enough, not for such a super-special godfather. So I hugged him good and hard.

"Thanks for loving her," I said, "and for so long a time." Then, for some reason, I said something akin to what Jo Silver had told me. "Sir, from now on, it's not my sky. It's yours, too."

Dr. Gray nodded. Then he spoke his last words to me in a hoarse whisper. "I owe you so much."

As I rolled up my sleeping bag, I saw my old prof start to climb the first ledge. I wanted to tell him that all of this was merely a clown's dream, because it was too bizarre, too comical, and only a circus act. Vaudeville video. It's a myth, because there isn't any Jo Silver Fox, no love story, and no happy ending. Back at school, Dean Stockton would never buy it, and he'd suspend me for skipping classes and getting high on a mountain.

How could anyone sane believe my story, or Jo Silver's or old Honest Abe's?

Dr. Gray climbed into the mist until he was out of sight and until my neck ached from watching, praying he'd make it. And then stay with her at Lost Pond, in love, forever and ever.

An old Romeo was scaling a granite balcony to his one and only Juliet.

20

I had heard the church bells of Sunday.

I'd been hiking rapidly, almost all day, most of it downhill, and, according to a helpful sun, headed due east.

The bells of a Sunday evening told me that I'd made it back. Pine Corners was dead ahead and I was alive. So was Dr. Abraham Gray and his Jo Silver. No, I thought, that was wrong. His beloved Johanah. I felt super about that, even though I was nearly insane with hunger and footsore fatigue.

It was dark when I hit town.

All the stores were closed and so was the Methodist Church. A few lights were burning in a house or two, here and there, houses which were almost all white, small, and now looking far more tidy in the dignity of darkness. I didn't know where to go. Mom used to say that there was a Guardian Angel to watch over Hollywood stuntmen and teenagers. As I spotted a name on the flank of a crooked mailbox, I knew Mom and the Angel worked on Sunday.

CLEPP, it read.

Even though his house was unlit, I boldly knocked. Inside somebody coughed, then clicked on a light. I also could hear a complaining voice muttering a disapproval of the hour, asking a yet ungreeted intruder what time it was. The door creaked open to reveal Mr. Clepp, in a rumpled gray-stripe flannel nightshirt, hooking his glasses over his ears.

"Yeah?" He grunted.

"It's me, Mr. Clepp. I'm back! And you were certainly right, sir. I couldn't find Lost Pond."

"Are you some kind of a nut? You woke me up to tell me *that*?"

I was hoping his welcome would be a degree or two warmer. Yet it hadn't been much less than reasonable, considering the hour and the arrival of a stranger. A porch light flicked on. "Who in the blazes *are* ya?" he growled.

"I'm Kenneth Matson."

"Who?"

"You remember. You sold me a compass last Wednesday."

"Well, whataya want...a refund? I warned ya that a compass don't function too proper up there."

I took a deep breath. "What I really want, Mr. Clepp, is something to eat, a place to sleep, and to use your telephone to call my parents."

Mr. Clepp snorted. "All *that*? I druther give you a *refund*. Or a good swift kick on yer hinder."

I couldn't help it. His Yankee hospitality just broke me up. As I tried to stand, laughing, I failed, then fell down in hysterics on the boards of his tiny porch. I was, I was thinking, no welcome picture of sanity.

"Okay. Come on in."

Inside, he turned on another light. Squinting at me

through his halfmoon bifocals, his eyebrows lifted in awe. "I ain't never," he groaned, "seen a pig as dirty as you."

"I'm sorry, Mr. Clepp. I'll pay you for your trouble. Honest."

"Cash. No credit."

"It's a deal." Mr. Clepp pointed a lean finger at the door. "Git outside and brush yerself off. Then come back in. But first, shake off some of them devil pitchfork prickers. You got more burrs on ya than three dogs."

I obeyed my host.

"The phone's in the kitchen."

I called home. The connection took several moments to complete. As I waited, Mr. Clepp opened an icebox that must have earlier belonged to Adam, stoked a big black stove, then fried me bacon and six eggs. I noticed that the toast was burning.

"Hello?" I heard Mom's voice, sounding as though she'd made a breathless dash to the telephone.

"Mom, I'm okay! I'm back in Pine Corners. Tomorrow morning, I'll catch a Trailways bus back to Lake Placid."

"Sam!" I heard her scream. "It's Kenny. Get on the other phone."

There were a hundred questions, for which I avoided rendering any truthful answers, because I wanted the secrets of Lost Pond kept from Mr. Clepp. Very little news, I presumed, came to Pine Corners, so the good hardware man might be tempted to share it. Not out of spite. Just gossip. Later, I'd explain everything to my parents.

Mr. Clepp straddled a chair backwards in the kitchen to watch me eat. He hadn't bothered to drain the bacon over a paper towel the way Mom did, but I wasn't about to complain. The toast was scorched black. Washed down with a glass of cold milk, however, the supper tasted super. I told him so.

"He ever find ya?" Mr. Clepp asked. "I mean that tall skinny school-teacher gent. He come to the store the day before yestiddy, all in a sweat of a haste, asking if I'd seen a strange kid. So did he find ya, or no?"

"Yes. He's on his way back to Lake Placid," I lied.

"Figured he'd locate ya. Or die lookin'. Had a firm clamp to his jaw, so I saw right away he'd discover where ya was." Mr. Clepp coughed. "You kin sleep on the sofa. It's so beat up that a mite more grime won't do no damage."

"Thanks, Mr. Clepp. I'll pay you for your trouble."

He shook his balding head. "No need." Then he changed his mind. "Well, maybe just fer the phone call. The chow's on the house. Z'at fair?"

I nodded. "More than fair." Smiling to myself, I knew that I had called on reverse and there would be no long distance charge on his bill. At least now I could reward his hospitality with a few dollars and not defy his friendship. It would not insult him.

"I gotta git to bed. G'night," he said. His bare feet, looking whiter than his sink, padded off. "Dang fool kid." He had no more to contribute.

Mr. Clepp's sofa, which some ancient upholsterer had stuffed with doorknobs, took a bit of adjusting to. But I was too bushed to care. Boots off, I lay well-fed in the dark, remembering. Perhaps by tomorrow, with luck, Honest Abe would reach his Johanah.

I thought about Amy Woodward. Maybe, next April, the two of us could take our spring vacation together and hike to Lost Pond. There were two very special people that I wanted her to meet and play her flute for.

"No," I whispered to the dark.

There was no longer a pressing need to return. Instead, we would find our own pond, sit under moonlight, and await the deer. I would hold Amy beneath my arm and shoulder, as Jo Silver would wish, and do one thing more.

Touch her nose to mine.

I dedicate this book to the wilderness of northern
New York State known as the Adirondack.

To every boy or girl who lies alone inside a sleeping bag, in darkness, many miles from home. And
to a memorable, strong-faced, white-haired lady
whom I met on a Montana mountain.

Her name is Sally Old Coyote.

Robert Newton Peck